Inklings Book 2015

Society of Young Inklings

The following young authors contributed their short stories and poems to this anthology.

Phoebe Barrientos

Benjamin Bouie

Kabir Aditya Buch

Sonia Cherian

Olivia Cisneros

Tal Dickman

Kiera Finlay

Rouli Freeman

Rachel Gould

Rachel Hoge

Mitesh Jain

Daniel Kao

Sonia Kulasooriya Camacho

Evie Landreth

Timothy Leung

Samantha Sasaki

Ashley Schwatka

Ellie Turk

Katie Turk

Cynthia Wang

Grateful acknowledgement is made to the following mentors for contributing their editorial guidance and letters.

Ann Jacobus

Briana Mitchell

Christine Dowd

Elizabeth Jellison

Erica McCuaig

Frances Lee Hall

Helen Pyne

Jena Brigantino

Kristi Wright

Laura Schmidt

Loraine McCormick

Mandy Davis

Marilyn Hilton

Melinda Cordell

Meridith Donahue

Naomi Kinsman

Patricia Pinedo

Patrick York

Sarah Rogers

Cover Illustration by: Brian Bowes, brianbowesillustration.com

Edited by: Briana Mitchell

Printed in the USA

First Printing: August 2015

ISBN: 978-0-9910031-6-7

Table of Contents

Poems

Special Thanks

The Inklings Book 2015 would not have been possible without generous gifts from:

San Benito Reality

Walters and Wolf

The Zanger Family

Society of Young Inklings also owes an enormous debt of gratitude to this year's Patron Society, writers and artists who gave from their hearts to support the work and dreams of these twenty inspiring young writers. Many thanks to:

John Austrian

Georgia Beaverson

Jena Brigantino

Miriam Busch

Bear Capron

Andrew Cochran

Mandy Davis

Erin Dealey

Marilyn Hilton

Ann Jacobus

Naomi Kinsman

Amy Laughlin

Lea Lyon

Peter Pearson

Helen Pyne

Evan Sagerman

Anne Schwab

David Shannon

Oriana Siska

Anne Ursu

Kristi Wright

Patrick York

Foreword

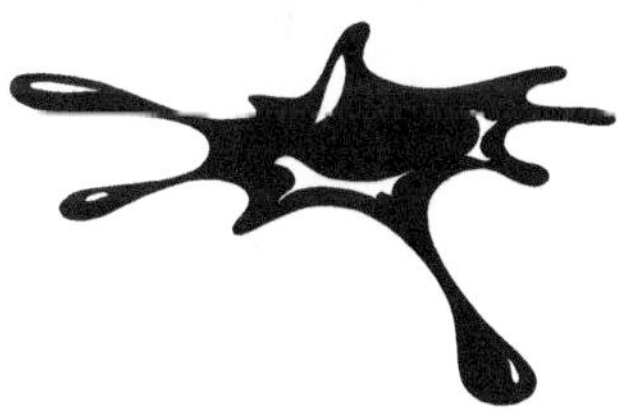

Imagine what it would be like if you could call yourself a published author by the eighth grade. The Inklings Book 2015 marks seven consecutive years of celebrating and publishing the work of young authors. Ranging all the way from first to eighth grade, this young generation of writers brings courage, inspiration, humor, and depth to their stories and poems. The pieces you are about to enjoy will inspire, challenge, and even tickle you silly!

We were overwhelmed and overjoyed by the quality and quantity of submissions this year. It wasn't easy, but after much deliberation, our editorial team chose twenty pieces for publishing. However, getting chosen was far from the last step! These authors embarked on a rigorous revision process designed to model what professional authors go through. Working closely with a Society of Young Inklings Mentor, each author chose a revision focus for their piece. After settling on a focus area, the authors and mentors worked side-by-side to bring out the strengths in their writing. With each submission, you will find a letter from the mentor explaining the revision focus for that piece, and even providing some fun tips for your own writing!

The Inklings Book 2015 highlights each writers' strength, and brings their writing to the next level. The stories and poems in this volume are arranged to showcase the wide variety these young authors have brought to this anthology. As you read, it is our hope that you will be inspired to dig deep in your own writing as well. If you find you just can't get enough, look for more fun tips, classes, and opportunities at www.younginklings.org.

Showing Instead of Telling

Loraine McCormick mentored Tal Dickman through a revision focused on using descriptive language and summary to move the story along in "My Grandfather's Singing Bowl."

Dear Reader,

Right from the start, I was intrigued by the premise of Tal Dickman's story, "My Grandfather's Singing Bowl." Tal's beautifully descriptive sentences and soulful imagery drew me into the world of Tibetan yak herders. His descriptions of the Himalayan landscapes were vivid and memorable, and he succinctly captured the feelings of terror and fear during the story's avalanche.

For this revision focus, we worked on showing and telling. Both are important to use when writing a story. When you show, the action slows down and the focus is on the little details. When you tell, you summarize the action of the story and things move along quickly.

When you are writing, think about looking at your story's world through a camera lens. When you zoom in, you magnify what you are seeing. You notice everything: the colors, the shapes, the smells, the emotions. You slow down the pace of the story. You use more dialogue. This is called showing.

When you zoom out, you're looking at your story from a broader perspective. Sometimes, to move the story along, the reader doesn't need to know about all the small details. The story moves at a very quick pace. You use little or no dialogue. Hours, years, and even centuries could fly by. This is called telling.

As a writer, you need to decide when you have written sufficient showing detail. Is the information that you are including moving the story along? Is this information really necessary to include? Will you lose the reader's interest if you include too much detail?

We worked on showing more of the main character, giving him a name (Chopak), and allowing him to interact more with his mother and father through external dialogue. We also gave Chopak internal dialogue (unspoken thoughts), which strengthens the reader's

emotional connection to him.

I asked Tal to remove information that went into detail about a Buddhist festival and to focus more on the singing bowl. The Buddhist festival was interesting, but not an integral part of this story. It would work better in a research paper. On the other hand, the reader wants to know more about the singing bowl and why it is so important to Chopak and his family, so Tal slowed down the action, showed more detail, and added more dialogue between the family members in which they discuss the history and importance of the singing bowl.

In one intense scene, the family is trying to escape, and there was an abundance of detail, long sentences, and a lot of dialogue. We backed off the camera lens and focused on telling, resulting in fewer details and shorter sentences. Dialogue was shortened to highlight the mother's anxiety and the main character's fear. The scene now moves rapidly, allowing the reader to really feel the intensity of the moment.

Our quest was to incorporate showing into Tal's story, as well as telling, and knowing when it's appropriate to employ which method. But how do you find the balance between showing and telling? What is too much and what is too little? When do you use the showing lens and when do you use the telling lens?

Ask yourself this: Are the details that I've included moving the story along, revealing character, or establishing the setting or the emotions? Am I showing enough?

Also ask yourself: In areas where the action needs to move more quickly, am I using fewer details, shorter sentences, and little or no dialogue? Am I telling enough?

"My Grandfather's Singing Bowl" now blends the important aspects of showing and telling, and I think you'll enjoy reading Tal's wonderfully creative story.

Happy writing!

Loraine

Loraine McCormick teaches

creative writing to children through the Society of Young Inklings. She has a B.A. in Advertising, with a concentration in English, from San Jose State University. She has worked in publishing as a copywriter and in high tech as a technical editor. Currently, she is writing several children's picture books, as well as a middle grade novel. She lives in San Jose, California, with her husband, two sons, and a golden doodle, Ginger.

13

Tal Dickman

My name is Tal Dickman. I am 10 years old. I live in the Bay Area and like to read, write, be with animals, play soccer, take Taekwondo, and swim. I live on a farm that has sheep, lambs, coy fish, dogs, cats, bunnies, chickens, and a lot of flies and bugs. That's me, Tal!

Here are some of Tal's thoughts on the writing and revision of "My Grandfather's Singing Bowl."

What changed in the story when you revised for showing instead of telling?

When I revised for showing, it made my story more interesting, and I think it will help the reader connect more with the main character, Chodak. My story now requires the reader to think more to interpret the story. I added dialogue, which allows my characters to interact with each other. I also worked on my main character's actions in a way that reflects his emotions at the time.

What did you learn from this process that you can use as you write your next story?

I will show important points, not just through dialogue but

also through actions. Next time I will try from the start to make a more satisfying book without holes in the plot, and to think about how the reader will connect with the story as much as possible. When something happens in the plot, I want to trigger the reader's emotions. In fact, I'm currently writing a book which is a character-driven story, where I switch perspectives so the reader can see different views of the main character to understand her better from the beginning. Most importantly, I will take the advice of an editor. Even though I might think that my story is good in the first draft, editing will help improve my writing.

What's your favorite part of My Grandfather's Singing Bowl?
My favorite part is when the main character, Chodak, runs away and cuts his leg on the boulder. He is forced to part with the only place he feels like he belongs. When I am sad, writing about depressing situations like this one makes me feel better. This makes me realize whatever is happening in my life is not the end of the world.

What was the hardest thing about the revision?
Knowing that the editor was right and had good suggestions. I really liked the way I had originally written my story, and I didn't think that anything needed to change. But, in the end, I knew that the edits would help.

What advice would you give other writers about revision?
It's important to be open-minded when you are working with an editor. I also found that it was important to show emotions changing throughout

the story. If you just focus on only one emotion (for instance, just happy or just sad), it makes that one emotion seem stale.

What inspired you to write about a singing bowl?

My teacher assigned a research project to my class. I had to pick one Tibetan artifact and write about it. My teacher has a singing bowl in the classroom, and I really like the sound and the shape of it. I like that you can keep a smooth calming sound going forever by moving the stick around the bowl. When my teacher showed me information about the Inklings writing contest, I decided to turn my school project into a story.

What are some of your favorite books?

The types of books I enjoy most are sad action novels. I can connect deeply with the characters when I feel as though I share traits with them. I also like historical fiction because I know that at one point in time there were people like that, and the historical details make the story more realistic. Just like in my own writing, it makes me feel better to know I am not in the worst position even when I am sad. Here is the list of some of my favorite books:

The Legend Trilogy-Marie Lu Chains and Forge by Laurie Halse Anderson
Persepolis by Marjane Satrapi
The Book Thief by Markus Zusak

My Grandfather's Singing Bowl

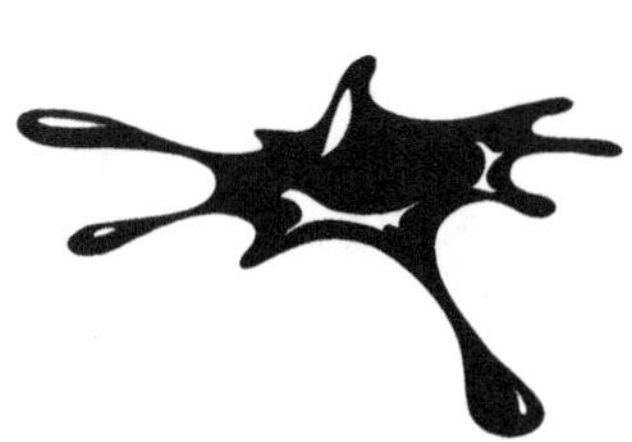

by

Tal Dickman

18

My eyes slowly opened, closed, opened, and closed. It's very hard for me to wake up in the morning. Inside the sleeping tent, the cold bit at my ears and scalp, but under my woolen blanket, I was warm.

Oh, just a few more hours of sleep, I thought.

But, just then, a loud, thunderous DONG shook the quiet morning awake. I knew that it was the sound of the singing bowl, my grandfather's singing bowl. It's the Tibetan bowl that my mother strikes every morning to wake the family.

I heaved myself up and out of my cozy cocoon.

"Come, Ngodup," I called to my dog.

His name means accomplishment, and he, well, smells like yak dung on an early Tibetan morning. A fetid, pungent smell. I pulled back the heavy tent flap and stepped outside. I looked toward the Himalayas in the east. The sun had just crested the top, and I squinted at the array of colors sprayed over the mountains. I shivered. Those mountains are beautiful on the outside, but dark and evil on the inside. I tried to ignore the uneasy feeling I had as I headed toward the cooking tent, where I could see my mother standing near the entrance.

"Nga-to delek, mother," I said. That means good morning in Tibetan.

"Nga-to delek," she said with a smile, as she ruffled my hair. "Here is the singing bowl and stick. Your breakfast is ready. You must eat enough for your long day with the yaks on the pasture."

I stepped inside the smoky, dusty tent. On the table, I could see a steaming bowl of tsampa porridge, which is made from roasted barley flour. Also, three Tibetan cups, dzabija, filled with tea sat waiting for us.

"Nga-to delek," my father greeted me warmly.

"And good morning to you, father," I said.

I quickly finished my breakfast and headed back outside. Today is Lha Bab Duchen, a special Buddhist celebration, and I must not be late for dinner.

"I wish you a good day," my mother said, handing me a dry piece of bread and some yak jerky for my lunch.

Ringing stick in one hand and bowl in the other, I hit the bowl and began to melt into its soothing tone, letting the sound resonate in my ears.

"Come, Ngodup," I said, as we headed to the yak enclosure to begin the morning herding.

We don't have names for our yaks, but I call my favorite yak William. One day, we were selling herbs and mushrooms at the trade market. We met an American man who was visiting. His name was William. The name grabbed my attention, not letting go. William the yak is big, warm, and comforting. He is a cloud on the ground, I imagine sometimes. His fur is the color of moonlight and his eyes the sun. Disrupting my daydream, Ngodup barked a ferocious, commanding bark, and the yaks turned in our direction.

"Good boy, Ngodup," I said.

William ran to me and stared into my eyes. He seemed alarmed, as if he sensed something coming.

"No, it must be just my imagination," I thought.

Again, I shook off the strange feeling. I whistled for the yaks, and they followed me past the gnarled roots and the beautiful mushrooms, which blurred and fused with the mahogany brown dirt. If it hadn't been for my grandfather, our family would not be living in these beautiful pastures. Instead, we might be in the ugly Tibetan camps where people are forced to live in concrete structures.

I belong to a family of yak herders. When my grandfather was young, he found a lone female yak in the mountains and started to care for it. Soon, he found a second yak, a male. The herd grew larger every year. We now have many yaks and a heavy milk production. We are not too skinny and we have enough to eat. The lives of these yaks depend on the flora around us. The trees and roots are plentiful, feeding our family and the yaks. In four days, though, we will say good bye to our beautiful summer pasture for another year. We will travel west to the winter pasture, which is 2400 meters down the mountain.

I have heard rumors that the Chinese government is against the Nomadic society of Tibet, so they are setting a policy. I'm not sure what that will be. I hope the government doesn't come to our pasture. We herders are used to the thin air and have no trouble breathing. For those who live at low elevations, it is almost impossible for them to breathe comfortably in our mountains. The elevation is too high for them

I returned to our tent at the end of the day, just as the sun was touching the ground. Ngodup raced back and forth around the yaks, while William remained right next to me. I hit the singing bowl to signal the yaks to their sleeping area. The singing bowl's tune always makes me feel something. The sound rings in my ears, but it's much more than that. The sound travels throughout my entire body and throughout my mind.

"Chodak," my mother called, startling me out of my thoughts. "Time to help make the momo."

"On my way, mother."

For dinner, my mother and I made momo and yak milk yogurt. Momo is a type of bread made from flour and water, usually with a meat, vegetable, or cheese filling. Momo is served on special occasions, like today, which is Lha Bab Duchen, a Buddhist festival celebrating the descent of Buddha from heaven to earth.

"Time to build the fire, Chodak," my father reminded me.

"Yes, father," I said.

One by one, I carefully stacked pieces of yak dung into the fire pit, quickly scraped a wooden match against a chunk of flint, and lit the pile of yak dung on fire.

"It makes me happy to see you build the fire for us," father said with a smile. "We are following the tradition of our nomadic ancestors."

I sat back and sighed. The musky smell of the yak dung was comforting, bonding my family with our ancestors who were here before us.

"A perfect time for the story of grandfather's singing bowl," my mother nodded toward my father, who was happily lost in thought.

It is a tradition that my father tells the story of my grandfather's singing bowl on this special day of Lha Bab Duchen.

"Ah, yes," my father said, nodding his head and placing his hand on his heart. "Grandfather's singing bowl. A long time ago, my father, your grandfather," he said, pointing to me, "found thousands of caterpillar fungi, but had no idea what to do with them. He kept them safe and dry in his tent. Ten weeks later, China invaded Tibet. One year later, Chinese traders arrived at his summer pasture. Grandfather showed them the caterpillar fungi, and the Chinese traders were excited. They offered your grandfather a block of brass for the fungi, which they said they used in Chinese medicines. Your grandfather then stacked the yak dung high in the outdoor fire pit. He made a huge fire. Huge. When the fire was big enough to be seen from miles away, he placed the block of brass in a ceramic bowl and melted the brass down into a liquid state. Then, wearing heat-resistant yak gloves, he shaped the brass into a bowl. This singing bowl. He then carefully etched Tibetan prayers into the brass. And here it is, the beautiful bowl."

Father then handed the bowl to me.

"Look how beautiful these etchings are," I said.

"Yes," mother agreed. "After all these years, it still brings us so much joy and appreciation."

"It is an important part of our family," said father, "and always will be."

I handed the bowl to mother, and after a few minutes, she returned it to father. He then took the wooden stick and gonged the bowl.

"Gonnnnnng." Father let the bowl ring long. It was a deep, rich tone. We listened carefully, absorbing the sound with our bodies, letting it resonate with a strong power.

With that beautiful sound soothing us and lulling us peacefully, we closed the evening in prayer and headed to our sleeping tent.

Four Days Later

In the middle of the night, a loud GONG broke the silence. Right away, I knew something was wrong. The tone was urgent. It was an alarm. My heart pounded quickly.

"Wake up!" my mother yelled.

"Mother, what's wrong?" I asked, shaking with fear.

"The Chinese government is coming. We must escape. We must hide in a place where they cannot go," my mother yelled over the whistling wind.

"But where?" I shouted.

Her answer sent a chill down my back.

"Where they cannot breathe as we can: the Himalayan Mountain Range."

I had heard stories about the mountains, and they were dark and frightening. Stories about people returning from the mountains with stubs for arms and lips that had lost their pigment.

The herders would argue.

"Those stories are lies," they would exclaim. Or they would say, "Don't scare the children!"

But I have seen Dorje, whose name means indestructible,

24

and he really was. He jumped off a mountain, he was so strong, or, at least, that was what the herders said. One day, he left his village, saying he was going to climb the Himalayas. A few months later, though, he returned with only three limbs, rasping that he didn't summit. His left arm was an ugly twisted knot of bone and flesh that couldn't even be called a limb, and he had a terrible case of hypothermia. The next day, he passed away in writhing agony. That memory was so terrible.

"But mother, remember Dorje," I said.

She just shook her sad, worried head.

"You must help us get ready now," she said sternly.

I didn't argue with her, but I didn't want to leave the pasture.

Nothing good will come if we climb up the mountain, I thought.

I was angry and scared. I grabbed the singing bowl and stick, put them into a knitted bag, slung it over my shoulder, and ran. I ran as fast as I could, away from the memories that had built a wall between our pastures and the peaks of the Himalayas. I ran until I could run no more. I sat down hard on a spiky boulder, piercing my leg and letting the rock draw blood as red as a Tibetan sunset.

"Oh, poor me, poor me, poor me," I cried.

But self-pity does nothing, so after a few minutes of nothing happening or going my way, I stopped crying and stood up. My bag caught on the jagged edge of the rock, and I angrily yanked it free. I solemnly walked back to the tent.

"Ho, heave, steady now," I could hear my father yelling at the yaks.

My father and mother were tugging and pulling the yaks' harnesses into place, gritting their teeth and grunting. I felt ashamed that I had not helped them. Soon, we headed toward the Himalayan mountains, leaving the pasture behind. No one said a thing about my disappearing or about the blood on my leg. My mother, though, gave me a knowing nod. I took one last look at the pasture, my eyes filling with tears and my throat tightening with anger. I got up on William the yak's back, leaned over and buried my face into the fur on his neck, and sobbed quietly.

Soon the excitement of the morning relaxed into the quiet rhythm of trotting yaks. But then, I had that uneasy feeling again. Suddenly, out of the silence there was a sharp CRACK. Then a RUMBLE. Moments later, the mountain behind us crumbled into a huge crevasse. Our only escape route was a small sliver of ice about one meter thick and one meter wide. There was no turning back. Just then, a loud CRACK rumbled right under our feet. The yaks surged forward like a pack of cheetahs. And the ground, where we had just been standing a moment before, suddenly gave way and crashed down the mountainside. I reached into my bag, which was still slung over my shoulder. I tried to pull out the singing bowl to calm the yaks, but my arm went straight through a hole. The singing bowl was gone!

"Ahhh!" I yelped, my heart pounding wildly. "I ripped my bag on that jagged rock! I was so busy feeling sorry for myself, and now grandfather's singing bowl is gone. I must find it," I yelled wildly.

I had to go back. I had to keep the family together, and the singing bowl tied us to my grandfather. Immediately, before my parents could react, I jumped off my yak and ran onto the sliver of ice. My safety was of no concern. Nothing mattered except for the bowl. Our bowl.

"Chopak, Chopak, where are you going?" yelled my father.

"Chopak, stop!" yelled my mother.

The sounds of my parents calling my name were soon quieted to a muffled sound that blew away in the wind. I was engulfed in a cloud. Quick thoughts were rushing in and out of my mind.

Go back, forget about the bowl. It's too dangerous.

And then, *Don't look down, don't look down.*

But deeper than those thoughts, I knew that I had to push on. The soothing sound of the singing bowl ringing in my head encouraged me. It was my driving force. As I was thinking, I became confused. I saw nothing below me, only clouds and patches of rock on the cliff side. All I remember is slipping and then I lost consciousness.

How much time passed, I didn't know. I woke clinging to the ice. And there they were, William and Ngodup.

"C'mon! We have to get the bowl," I yelled, as I took William by the harness and led him down the mountain.

Time passed with no value. The minutes seemed like hours, and the hours seemed like days. We moved carefully along the sliver of ice, and, thankfully, it gradually widened. There was a small break in the clouds, and I could see our summer pasture. And there was the singing bowl, right at the point where the pasture met the mountainside.

"There it is!" I yelled at the top of my lungs.

I could feel its energy. I could hear its sound. The feeling was overwhelming, comforting like the love of a parent when you are full of sorrow. I ran to the bowl and held it to my heart, tears streaming down my face. Holding on tightly to the bowl, I climbed onto William's back and turned him toward the mountain. I stared at the stars twinkling and the last rays of sun highlighting the horizon. Triumphantly, Ngodup pointed his snout to the sky, sniffed, and then slowly started to follow a scent. He then went faster and faster. William and I followed in procession, and before long, I could hear voices.

"Chodak! Where are you?" called my mother.

Again, I could see only clouds.

"Is that you? Chodak?" my father yelled.

"Mother?"

"Father?"

We ran to each other's arms, embracing tightly, not wanting to let go. They are my family. They are my light. And my grandfather's singing bowl keeps us together.

Upping Tension in the Climax

Meridith Donahue worked with Phoebe Barrientos to add a little extra drama to her story by focusing on creating tension in the climax of "Simple Magic."

Dear Reader,

Phoebe Barrientos's "Simple Magic" will take you on a journey to a world of fairies, magical railways, and a school where a ringing bell announces your magical ability. I guarantee you'll want to stay there, exploring and conversing with the wonderful creatures you meet.

Phoebe brings her setting to life through imaginative, specific details that draw the reader into her world. Since her setting is so strong, I wanted the reader to feel the excitement and tension of the main character, Karen, on her journey to Stellar Dreams, School of Magic. Phoebe and I began work on upping the drama in the climax.

Each scene in a story builds on the one before

it. The climax is the most exciting moment in the story, when the main character faces her biggest challenge. This important scene needs to be balanced—not fly by too fast or creep along too slowly—so the reader stays interested in the story.

I wanted Phoebe to slow down and add a few more details so that Karen's conflict was more apparent—it is Karen's self-doubt that brings about the story's climax. By adding some specific character and sensory details, the story's climax came to life.

To do this, Phoebe and I modified an Inklings game called Six-Sided Where. She pretended she was an outside observer to the climax of her story, and I asked her questions about what she saw, heard, felt, smelled, and tasted. Most importantly, I wanted her to focus on Karen and how her self-doubt shows outwardly— twisting her hair or staring at her shoes, for example. These actions are called business, which is something a character does that shows how she feels inside.

Phoebe did an excellent job of exploring her setting and character to add drama. She sprinkled in the perfect amount of detail to add suspense as Karen faces her big challenge.

Do you need help upping the drama in your story's

climax? Does the story's climax go too fast or too slow? If you need to slow the pace down, consider playing Six-Sided Where. Close your eyes and pretend you are a detective, observing your main character and taking note of all the sensory details you can. If your scene goes by too slowly, read through it again. Where does the action slow down? Are there details that aren't as important as others? Cut those sentences out and see how the action flows. Remember, small changes can make a big impact.

Most importantly, have fun! Making changes to your story can seem overwhelming, but if you take it slowly and set small goals for yourself, you'll be happy with your revision.

Happy writing,
Meridith

Meridith Donahue has an MFA in Writing for Children and Young Adults from Hamline University. She loves being an Inklings instructor and is hard at work revising her young adult novel.

Phoebe Barrientos

Phoebe is a fifth grader at Duveneck Elementary school. When not writing, she can usually be found reading. She has a Manx cat and also enjoys playing video games and playing with her brother.

Here are some of Phoebe's thoughts on the writing and revision of "Simple Magic."

Do you like revision?

I like revision because it gives you the chance to go back to your story and add more, because I always feel rushed to finish my story. Right then, I don't want to add any more, but after a little time, I feel like I could have put so much detail in and revision gives me the chance to do it.

What advice do you have for other Inklings who don't like revision very much?

If you feel like you want to finish really quickly, it's easy to finish your story and then go back and add a lot of detail and extra stuff you didn't write before. It's a lot easier knowing that you've already written the end.

What was the best part of writing "Simple Magic"?
I liked how I could do what I wanted with it, because I could just say that the characters used magic and it would make sense, because the possibilities are pretty much endless.

How did you get the idea for your story?
I just went with it! I wanted to write a story with magic in it because I really like fantasy, and I wanted it to have a message. I think that makes the writing sound better.

What gave you the idea for the hierarchy of magical creatures?
I started out with the first sentence, and then I thought it would be boring if the amount of magic the creatures all had was random. I wanted to come up with some way to order it, and the hierarchy seemed like the most convenient.

Do you think endings are the hardest to write? Why?
Yes. It's hard to figure out a good way to end. It should give a sense of completion and it can be really hard to find a sentence that actually works. If you like your story so much that you don't want to end it, that's also hard. But it's not hard if you've already created a [plot] map.

Where do you like to write?

I like to write in sunny places where I can sit and be warm, and also where no one else is coming and bothering me. Then I don't get a lot written.

Do you like to read? What are your favorite books?

I really like reading. I like the *Septimus Heap* series by Angie Sage, and it's all about magic and fantasy. I also like funny books, because if there's no humor, then it's not always very good.

Do you have any other recommendations for fantasy books?

I just read *The Wish Stealers* and it's about a girl who is trying to use magic while she's still in everyday life. She bought a box of pennies and each of the pennies represented a wish that someone had. The wishes had been stolen, and the girl tries to return the wishes to their original owners.

Do you ever feel stuck? What do you do?

Yeah, I get stuck a lot. I run out of ideas, because I just start writing without a plan for how I'll tie it up. I like to create a plan of what's going to happen. With this story, I made a time line. I also like to plan scenes.

Simple Magic

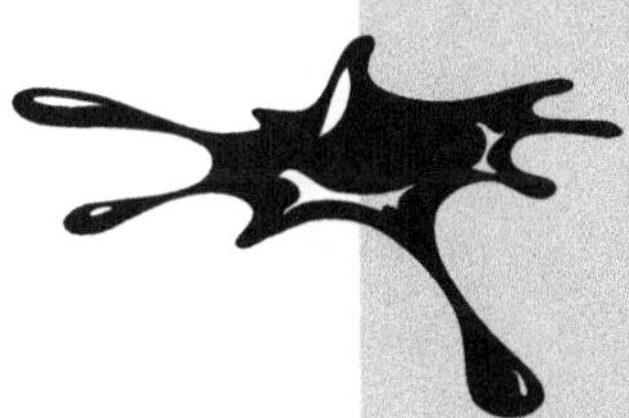

by

Phoebe Barrientos

36

"Everyone has a bit of magic in them. That magic is what makes the stars twinkle at night and ripe fruits smell sweet. It makes all the little things that make people feel good happen, and there's some in you too."

Karen would smile when her grandfather told her that each night. Although she was a human, the species with the least magical potential, she was almost obsessed with the enchanting subject of magic, just as her Grandad was. He had worked as a wizard's assistant when he was younger, and he had learned a lot about it then.

One day as she was picking up the mail while demonstrating her usual respect for the unique pelican who delivered their mail (Grandad said they stored a great deal of magic in their big beaks), Karen noticed a silvery envelope among the regular whites and yellows. Wow!

"Hey Mom, I think you got a magical letter. Isn't that cool?"

"Can I see?" her mother asked.

She was trimming Karen's younger brother, Anthony's, hair.

"Karen, this is addressed to you," she said after a look, her eyebrows rising slightly.

"What? Karen got a magic letter? That's not fair!" exclaimed Anthony, jerking forward.

His mom sighed. She would have to trim the back even shorter now.

Karen pushed her dark, wavy hair out of her face and looked closely at the letter. Her mother was right! *Karen Atlereen*, the letter read. With a smug grin at her brother, she snuck upstairs to her room to read it.

Upon opening the letter, a fluff of golden dust escaped and zipped past Karen, stopping in the center of her bedroom. Magic dust! Grandad said wizards used it for more complicated spells, like magical letters. Karen watched as the tiny particles formed themselves into words, and when the enchanting display was finished, a complete message hung suspended in the middle of her room.

"Amazing." Karen whispered, and began to read the letter.

Dear Miss Karen,

Recently, it has come to my attention that you are a human with extraordinary magical potential. You may just be skilled enough to attend a school of magic, and I would be delighted if you chose my academy, Stellar Dreams. There is a wonderful environment here, and the school is located directly next to a forest filled with magical creatures. I hope you will join. If so, catch the Twinkletoes Railway on May 19 at 1:00 p.m. and show them this letter.

Swervin Mervin,

Principal of Stellar Dreams, School of Magic

Everything seemed to shine with new possibilities.

Me? Go to a magic school? Karen thought. *That's impossible. Maybe it's a prank.*

But when she took out the paper copy of the letter she knew came with every magical one, Karen realized it couldn't be a prank. It had Swervin Mervin's unmistakable magical signature. All wizards left one behind when they signed something, and each was unique in its own way. It was really true. Karen could go to a magical school, and the principal of Stellar Dreams – one of the greatest magical academies in the world – wanted her.

Karen's parents had been skeptical about it at first. "What if you're not magical enough? You're only a human." "It's so far away…." "Magic can be dangerous!"

But they had no choice but to let her go when Grandad heard the news. He had countered every doubt with his vast knowledge of magic. Good old Grandad. He understood how much Karen wanted to go.

"Besides," he said, "Who knows more about magic than Karen?"

"Nobody but you, Grandad," she had replied with a grateful smile.

The Twinkletoes Railway was known throughout the world for its extraordinary method of travel. It created shining tracks for itself out of thin air, sucking the magic it used to make them back up after traveling over the silver rails. The best part though, was that the tracks would lift the train into the air, allowing the freedom of the sky to travel through. Grandad used to give Karen rides on his shoulders, pretending that she was riding the Twinkletoes Railway, but now she was taking a trip on the real one. The ticket seller had immediately given Karen a first-class ticket when she pulled out her letter. Now she was sitting in a soft chair and gazing down on tiny cottages below.

When the magical train finally pulled into a special stop next to Stellar Dreams, Karen was beginning to have doubts about her magical ability. She was a human, and they almost never had enough magical ability to wield it.

Almost never, Karen, she told herself. *But you do. Swervin Mervin said so; it has to be true!*

She found herself chewing on her hair and hurriedly pulled it out of her mouth. How many times had Anthony teased her about it?

"You only chew on your hair when you're nervous!" he had told her.

Inwardly, Karen scolded herself. *Why should you be nervous? You wouldn't even be here if you weren't magical.*

But soon her attention was diverted to a scene at the edge of the trees lining the walkway.

"Hey! Get away! Stop pulling my hair, would you?!" A small fairy was trying to get away from a trio of imp-like gristles, or fairy barbers, as Grandad called them.

Although they had even less birth magic than the average human, gristles could gain it by pulling a fairy's hair out, which unfortunately, is a fairy's main magic center. This fairy's vibrant blue braids sparkled as she struggled to get away from the gristles. Karen rushed over to the creatures and swatted them away from the fairy with the travel brochure she had picked up on the Twinkletoes Railway.

"Thank you, thank you!" She flitted up to Karen's height.

Not surprisingly, the excited fairy shone with magic, fairies being arguably the most magical species around.

"They almost got me that time! I'm Penelope, and I really owe you one, Karen!"

Karen didn't ask how Penelope knew her name. Fairies had a strange way of knowing things. It was best not to question it.

"You seem pretty magical. And yet you're a human. I guess you're a special case. Are you going to this school?" Penelope indicated Stellar Dreams with a wave of her skinny arm.

"I'm new, but I will" replied Karen. *I hope*, she added to herself, although she tried not to.

Then she said good-bye to Penelope and walked back towards the school, again doubting her magical talent.

Ding, dong. The bell! Suddenly Karen remembered the most special thing about Stellar Dreams. Above the arch leading into the school building hung a beautiful silver bell. When someone with enough magical ability passed under the arch, the bell would ring. It was an unspoken rule that to go to the school, you had to make the bell ring. Oh no.

No, it's okay, Karen tried to tell herself. *Of course you have enough magical ability! Didn't Penelope just tell you?*

But try as she might, she couldn't drive the doubts from her mind. And as she walked through the giant arch, the world seemed completely quiet, and the bell stayed still.

The color drained from Karen's face as she stood there rooted to the spot, afraid to take another step. She didn't cry or even make a sound, but her stomach collapsed and her legs trembled like two thin trees in the wind.

Nobody seemed to notice Karen as she walked into the building. Everyone was eating lunch and chatting with their friends. There were unicorns, elves, and even folk who looked like humans, but had butterfly wings sprouting from their backs. Lots were practicing and studying magic. Although many strange creatures were milling about, Karen was the only one who felt out of place.

"You just walked in? We're having lunch hour." A couple of students walked up to her. "Hey, um, why didn't the bell-"That was it.

Karen ran out of the building and into the cover of the trees. Now tears flowed freely down her cheeks, all her contained disappointment rushing out. Her sneakers crunched on the dry leaves that littered the forest floor. Suddenly she stopped, face-to-face with a surprised blue-haired fairy.

"Karen, what's the matter?" Penelope asked. "Shouldn't you be at school?"

"I would… if I had enough magic."

"The bell didn't ring? But you have lots of magic. We just need to wake it up. Come on."

Karen tried not to raise an eyebrow. The bell hadn't rung. There was no point in pretending it could have. But nevertheless, she silently followed her new friend as a sour frown raced across her face.

Penelope led her deep into the forest until they reached a tree with a six-pointed star engraved on it. She touched the star, and it started to glow. Suddenly, lights of all colors burst out of the tree. Karen felt light as a feather.

"What are these?" Karen's tear stained cheeks quickly

dried in the comforting warmth that suddenly enveloped her like a blanket. Her eyes grew wide with amazement. The next moment, a cool calm washed over her as a blue light floated past her. With each new light that came close to her, a new feeling came over her, all of them helping Karen get over her initial shock.

"These special lights wake up magic. But sleeping magic wasn't the only thing that didn't work for you when you walked through the arch." Penelope settled herself on a fallen log. "It wasn't just magic you were filled with when I met you. I also saw doubt. Those two things don't mix. Magic will sometimes refuse to show itself when you're not sure it's there. But still, don't get too full of yourself. You haven't even started school. Now it's time for you to ring that bell." She said with a warm smile.

Karen smiled with her. Wow! After seeing these lights, Karen felt much better. It was much easier to believe what Penelope said with a clear mind and better mood. Karen had been so doubtful when she had walked under the arch. She even remembered Grandad telling her something of the sort, now that she thought about it. Why hadn't she remembered before?

Karen had no doubts this time when she walked through the arch. She knew that although she may not have as much magic as some of the people milling about inside the school, she had more knowledge, thanks to Grandad, and more trust, because of Penelope.

And from above, she heard the clear ring she'd been waiting for.

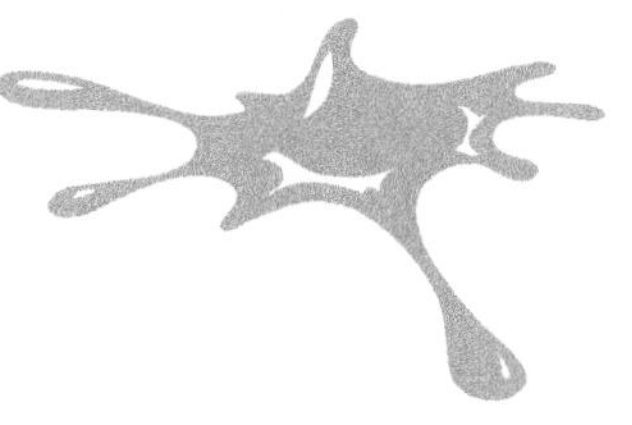

44

Descriptive Language

Christine Dowd mentored Ellie Turk through a revision focused on using descriptive language to evoke specific images in her story, "Just a Rose."

Dear Reader,

I very much enjoyed reading "Just A Rose." I think that the story has a very nice message and I also think Ellie does a good job of describing the roses.

In this revision, we focused on description. For example, "…They all shone in the afternoon sun glistening with droplets of dew that hadn't yet gone." This is a lovely sentence. Using very few words, Ellie gives the reader a vivid sense of the roses. I can see them and I can see the dew on their petals. In the next sentence she mentions their fragrance. This is very nice because she is using the senses to evoke an image for the reader. Since this is one of her strengths as a writer, I thought it might be a good idea to focus on her descriptions in the story and play them up even more. We looked at three main principles in our revision.

FIRST: Sometimes less is more. Sometimes one strong verb or adjective can be enough to evoke an image for the reader. Sometimes, using too many words, or adjectives, can have the opposite effect and bog down the sentence.

SECOND: When revising, we thought about ways to avoid repeating the same word twice in sentences that are close together. For instance, if she used the word 'rose' in a sentence then she avoided repeating that word again in the next sentence.

THIRD: I think that this story has a lot of depth. I like that roses are important to Rebecca and that they symbolize what is valuable to her in her life. I wanted to know why Rebecca feels so strongly about them. I asked Ellie to consider adding a couple of sentences after Rebecca sees the house on Maple Lane. We know that she

gets her appetite back, but what is it about the roses that she connects to?

I think Ellie has a wonderful story here, I hope you enjoy reading "Just a Rose."

Happy Writing,
Christine

Christine Dowd

Growing up in a bilingual home in which French was spoken as much as English, contributed to Christine's appreciation for the subtle nuances of language. From an early age, she has always been attracted to the sounds of words and how they can be linked in a fluid way. Christine has taught ninth and tenth grade English and French. Currently, she works as a mentor for young writers for the Society of Young Inklings in the San Francisco Bay Area. She graduated from VCFA's WCYA program in 2013. Christine is an avid horseback rider and likes to draw parallels between writing and riding dressage. Like all art forms, both can be continually taken to a higher level. There is no such thing as perfection. While there may be harmonious moments that bring the rider a sense of elation, these moments are fleeting and can only be regained through practice. Similarly, a writer crafts a story until it flows so smoothly that it looks deceptively easy. Both writing and riding are subtle arts that require developing a 'feel for' - skills that require you do more with less.

Ellie Turk

Ellie was born and raised in California. She has enjoyed writing since she was four years old. Her favorite genre is fiction, because you can write about anything, even magic. Ellie keeps active with swimming, softball, basketball, and soccer. She also plays the piano and is a Girl Scout. Ellie has a poster in her room that says, "She leaves a little sparkle everywhere she goes" – a statement couldn't be more true of this vivacious and energetic young writer.

Here are some of Ellie's thoughts on the writing and revision of "Just a Rose."

Why do you like to write?

I like writing because you can take the story any way you want.

Was there anything that surprised you during the revision process?

Not really, at least not yet at least.

What's your favorite part in "Just A Rose"?

I like the part when Rebecca sees the roses. I think I wrote it very well and it really brings the picture to life.

How did you get your idea to write "Just A Rose"?

I don't know. It just popped into my head and I started writing.

Do you have any favorite books you would recommend to other writers and readers?

Yes, two series actually. *Wings of Fire* by Tui T. Sutherland and *Amelia Rules* by Jimmy Gownley.

50

Just A Rose

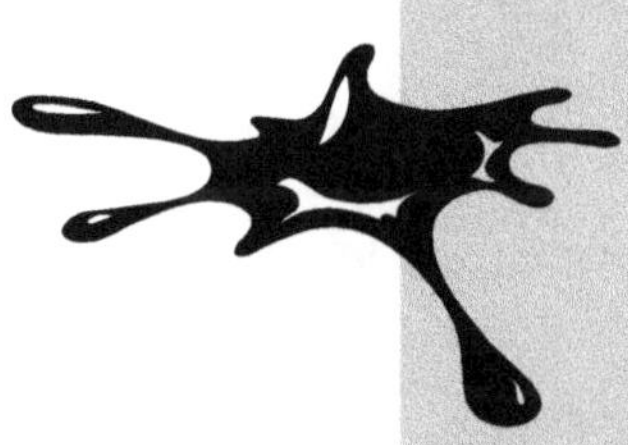

by

Ellie Turk

52

Rebecca White had never been exactly specific on what she wanted people to do when she died.

Her mother, Mrs. White, said, "Honey, you have a long time to decide. You're only nine!"

Rebecca replied stubbornly, "I want to be ready."

"I want a party in my honor..." proclaimed Rebecca's little brother, Tom. "And also a planet named after me!"

Rebecca shrugged and turned away.

At the dinner table, Rebecca just poked at her steak with her fork.

"What's wrong with your steak?" asked Mr. White. "Your mother made it especially for you."

Rebecca shrugged and silently ate a few bites of food. When it was time for bed, she felt quite sick and couldn't sleep. Rebecca didn't even close her eyes that night.

The very next morning, the same thing happened. Rebecca ate

almost nothing, but her mother sent her off to school and called Dr. Redmann.

"Who is it?" asked Dr. Redmann's scratchy voice. "Not Mr. Peacock, I hope? I'm not giving you the medicine yet."

"No, not at all, Doctor," Mrs. White said in a worried tone. "It's Barbara White. I'm calling about Rebecca. She hasn't eaten anything except a tiny bit of toast, steak, peas, or cereal in two days."

Dr. Redmann paused. "Two days! That's not healthy for a growing girl like Rebecca. Perhaps she has something on her mind."

Mrs. White gasped. Maybe Rebecca was so busy thinking about what she wanted people to do in her honor when she was dead that she wasn't eating!

"Thanks, Doctor. I appreciate your help," she said happily. Now she could help Rebecca!

Later, in the driveway, Mr. White was revving up the car. Its old engine sputtered and spit.

"Come on, Dad!" shouted Tom. "I want to go to Peter's Pizza Palace!"

Rebecca groaned as the car finally pulled out of the driveway.

"Are you okay, Rebecca?" asked Mr. White, turning the rearview mirror so that he had a clear view of his daughter.

"No," complained Rebecca. "My stomach hurts."

Tom grinned so that his teeth ached. "I bet you a million trillion quadrillion dollars that you're hungry!"

Mr. White drove the car into the parking lot of Pete's Pizza Palace. "Well, maybe some pizza will fill you up. Along with some ice cream."

Tom bounced up and down. "Yaaaay! Ice cream!"

Rebecca rolled down her window and stared at the house across the street.

Its address was 2517 Maple Lane. Beautiful roses surrounded the house.

Some were pink, some red, and some white. They all shone in the afternoon sun, glistening with droplets of dew that hadn't yet gone.

The roses looked soft and comfortable. Someone had cut off their thorns, and they were by far the most beautiful, colorful roses Rebecca had ever seen.

Through the open window of the car, Rebecca could smell the fragrant aroma of sweet-smelling roses. Rebecca sighed happily and listened to the bees buzzing around the roses.

The roses cheered Rebecca up immediately, and that night, when Mrs. White talked to Rebecca about her eating habits, Rebecca had eaten a large pizza and felt quite full.

Fifty-three years later, Rebecca now lived in the house surrounded by roses. She spent so much time out in her garden tending the roses that anyone passing by thought she was a nutcase, because Rebecca even cared for her garden in winter. "She'll get sick eventually," said a man. "Just wait and see."

During the winter, Rebecca caught a bad case of double pneumonia.

She died three weeks later.

And when her will was read, all it said was:

Just A Rose

Rebecca's son, Lucas, claimed those were the last words that she said.

People came from near and far to donate roses. Everywhere, people remembered Rebecca's last words. People from Alabama, the Bahamas, Missouri, England, Russia, Austria, California, Mozambique, Egypt, Cuba and any other place you can imagine sent roses.

If Rebecca were still alive, she would have been very pleased.

By the end of the rose craze, people from Rebecca's town erected a statue with a plaque that said:

REBECCA WHITE

ALL SHE WANTED WAS A ROSE

And citizens of the town remembered Rebecca, and how she asked for only what she needed to keep her happy.

And no one in the town forgot Rebecca White.

She got her last wish.

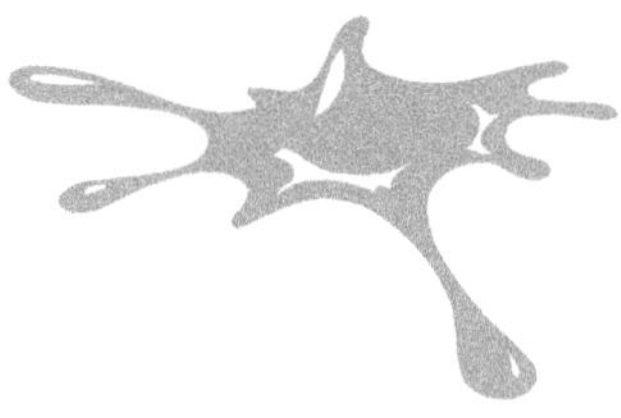

Showing Character Motivation through Dialogue

ena Brigantino mentored Mitesh Jain through a revision focused on developing his characters' voices through the use of dialogue.

Dear Reader,

Mitesh's story "The Vegetarian Lion" is a wonderful story reminiscent of a fable. (A fable is a story typically featuring animal characters that teaches a moral or lesson). Mitesh's main character, the lion, is very memorable and brave.

In his revision, Mitesh focused on showing character motivation through dialogue. Readers should be able to relate to characters so they can understand their motivation later on in the story. Adding character-specific dialogue brings readers even closer to your characters.

Mitesh's first draft was well developed with a solid beginning, middle and end. I already felt connected to the main character. However, I wanted to know more about the lion and his feelings. I also wanted to know more about the other characters, too. I wanted to hear their voices.

Adding lines of dialogue for multiple characters can be difficult. But that's just what Mitesh did in his revision. Not only did Mitesh add dialogue for the main character, he also added dialogue for the secondary characters, which added even more depth to the relationships in the story. As you read "The Vegetarian Lion" think about what you learn about each character from what they say.

One strategy to give a character more dialogue in stories is to ask yourself, "why does this character feel this way?" Then ask yourself "what could this character say aloud to show this feeling?" If your character is alone consider using internal dialogue.

Another strategy is to put yourself into your character's shoes. Ask a teacher, parent or friends to

interview you as that character. Answer the questions as your character would. You'll be surprised at what you learn.

Happy Writing!

Jena

Jena Brigantino

grew up playing outdoors in central California where she dreamed up stories featuring animals. Jena wishes she had the opportunity to take an Inklings class as a child. She strives to extend the opportunity to as many children as possible. Jena began working with Society of Young Inklings as an intern in 2010. She holds a B.A. in Creative Arts and a minor in Education from San Jose State University. She also holds units in Early Childhood Development. She's worked with children of all ages teaching dance, theatre arts, and creative writing classes. Jena loves collaborating with such a creative team at SYI.

Mitesh Jain

Mitesh was born in Boston, MA, to a Polish mom and an Indian dad. From a very early age, he had a great interest in letters, sounds and books. Besides his first name, the very first words he learned to spell were "computer" and "chocolate." Mitesh loves writing and is passionate about all kinds of sports, especially baseball. Any chance he gets, he wants to practice throwing, catching, pitching, bouncing, dribbling or tossing a ball — outside, in a garage, even in his living room! He is currently in first grade at Almond Elementary School in Los Altos, CA. Besides sports and the Red Sox, Mitesh loves animals (especially lions and tigers), vanilla ice cream, and his two little brothers, Kavi and Kuba. He and his family are vegetarian.

Here are some of Mitesh's thoughts on the writing and revision of "The Vegetarian Lion."

When did you start writing?

When I was four years old. My first book was written on a piece of cardboard and was only two pages. It was called "The Mouse Went into the House."

Where do you like to write?

At home on my blue table, when I am full of ideas.

How do you come up with story ideas?

I get some of my ideas from my dreams and other TV shows.

How do you feel about the revision process?

I feel proud of the revisions I made on "The Vegetarian Lion." The difficult part was coming up with what the other animals would say when teasing the lion. First, I came up with a list of things that a real lion does. Then, I made a list of opposites. The third step was putting the mean things into a sentence.

What advice do you have for other Inklings, especially if they don't like revising very much?

If you revise you will get a better story. I would also ask a teacher or parent to read your story.

62

The Vegetarian Lion

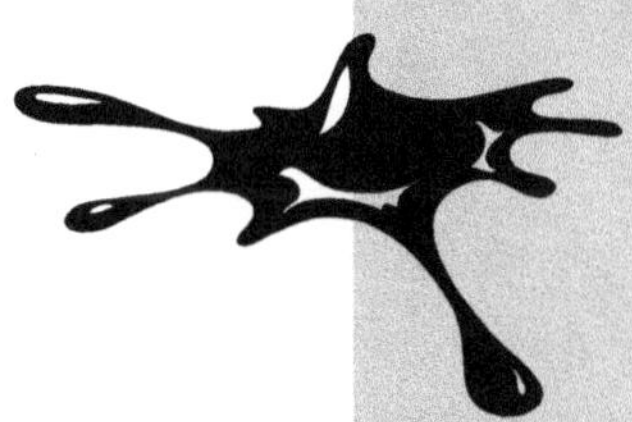

by

Mitesh Jain

64

Once upon a time there was a vegetarian lion. The lion had an orange mane, a slim, yellow back and very sharp teeth. Every day the lion got teased by gazelles, giraffes, and zebras because he was vegetarian.

Zebras said, "Maybe you are too old to chase animals. That's why you're vegetarian."

Gazelles said, "You are too slow to catch a fast gazelle."

Giraffes said, "Are you not powerful enough to roar? We are not scared of you at all."

The lion did not like the way the animals teased him.

He said to them, "You are so mean. Stop teasing me."

But the animals did not listen. They kept making fun of him.

"You are so thin because you only eat leaves," they teased him. "Maybe you can't chew meat because you don't have any teeth," they laughed. "You are too nice to be a lion."

The lion felt sad that the animals did not respect him. He walked away and sat behind a tree and looked at the sky. He was upset but still he did not want to hurt the animals.

* * *

Then one day a group of bad people came to the savanna. They started throwing trash, cutting down trees and pulling out bushes. The animals watched in horror and felt sad because their habitat was being destroyed.

The lion did not see this because he was sitting behind the tree feeling sad and lonely. Suddenly, the bad people pulled out guns and started shooting the animals. When the lion heard the big "ra-ta-ta-tat" sound of the guns, he raced to see what was going on.

He saw trash all around, bushes out of the ground and tree stumps all over. He saw the animals running in all directions. They looked very scared. The lion felt that he needed to save the animals.

He said to the hunters, "Hey, stop trying to shoot those animals," in a powerful voice, but the hunters ignored him.

The lion felt really angry. He took a deep breath, scratched the dirt with his giant claws, and let out the loudest, most powerful roar anyone has ever heard. The lion's roar was so loud that it shook the entire savanna. The hunters got so scared that they dropped their guns and quickly ran away.

The animals cheered and danced.

They said, "Thank you," to the lion in such a gracious manner because they were so thankful. They also said "Sorry for teasing you. We will never do it again."

They even gave him a medal made out of sticks and leaves

to show that he was their hero. From then on, everyone respected him. They even threw him a party for helping them.

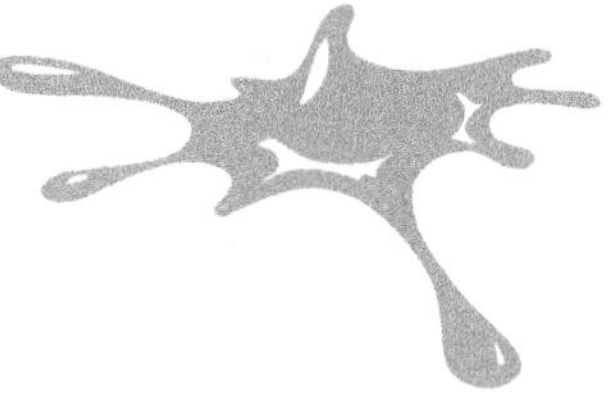

68

Cause and Effect

Patricia Pinedo mentored Rouli Freeman through a revision focused on using cause and effect to develop character interactions.

Dear Reader,

The story, "The Five Little Mice and The Cat," will be a fantastic addition to the Inklings Book 2015. I was excited to work with Rouli on the revision process.

In this revision, I focused with Rouli on cause and effect. In other words: Why do the mice and cat interact the way that they do in the story? Throughout the plot, Rouli used great situations, but at times they distracted from the interactions of the mice and cat.

The situations in his story led me to believe that this tale would benefit from more description and reasons that lead up to the final parts of the story. In other words, we tried to develop reasons to explain why the cat and mice do what they do in the story.

Since Rouli is strong at creating details, we focused on using those details very strategically.

First, I asked him to explain more about how the characters feel during certain moments of the story. For example, when the cat couldn't get into the tree house, how did he feel? Upset, frustrated, sad? I had Rouli look at these moments and see how he could identify and show his characters' feelings.

Second, we worked on using more details in the way he presented certain settings. For example, the part where Rouli talks about the auto playground is very interesting, but I suggested that perhaps we could use that level of detail in other places in the story, such as to describe the tree house more.

Third, because endings are so important, we added more detail there, as well. Rouli described how the mice continued to build the playground for people and how the people used it to their advantage.

Notice that by adding more details, more lingering questions can be answered for the person who reads the story.

Storytelling is an art form that takes a lot of

passion and dedication. Writers have the opportunity to create memorable, fun characters that readers will want to read over and over again. Writing is a great form of expression that many people enjoy as a way of explaining or escaping the reality around them

I am very impressed with Rouli's story. I think it is a fantastic piece and I am excited to see the finished work. Congratulations again, Rouli, on your story.

Happy Writing,
Patricia

Patricia Pinedo earned her B.A. in Literature with an emphasis in Creative Writing-Poetry from UC Santa Cruz. Her poetry has been published in literary journals. She completed her Masters in Fine Arts in Creative Writing at San Jose State. She has been a substitute teacher for the past four years, and has worked with a wide range of grade levels. Patricia is excited to be working with Society of Young Inklings, helping young students develop their storytelling and writing skills.

Rouli Freeman

Rouli is an energetic second grade home-schooler. He loves reading books, writing and playing Minecraft. He writes short stories often.

Here are some of Rouli's thoughts on the writing and revision of "Five Little Mice and the Cat."

What did you expect to change when we started adding more details to your story?

I am not too sure. Like lots of grammar fixes. And some parts less explanation and some parts more explanation.

Did you like how the story changed?

Yeah.

Do you think the revision made your story better?

Yeah!

Do you like to tell stories?

I used to do that.

What would you like to tell other kids about writing?

Do not do it if you don't want to.

What was your favorite part of this story to write?

I liked where I made up this part about how they got water from a tree. Because when I described the tree house, I had a part where they got water and I added that they got water from a button in the wall of the tree.

Who was your favorite character in your story?

The five little mice. They don't have the little hairs.

What else are you working on?

I also have a very short story collection too. Very small stories.

74

Five Little Mice
and the Cat

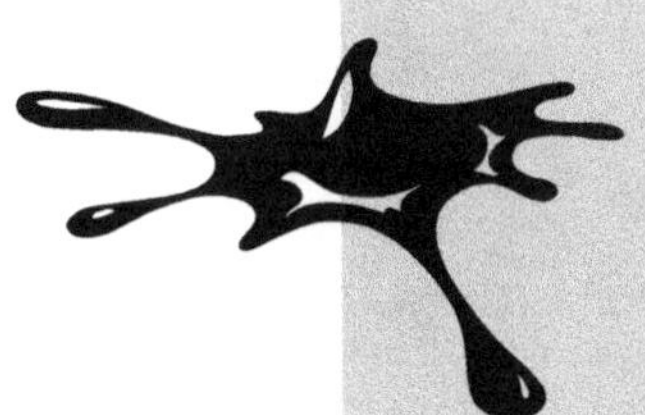

by

Rouli Freeman

76

CHAPTER ONE

Once upon a time, there were five little mice. When they were old enough to live by themselves, they found five trees and they made five tree houses inside the tree trunks. They were completely hidden except for five small knots that you could pull to open the five doors. Inside the doors, there were locks that made each knot un-pullable.

There were five very tall ladders that went up to each room. In each of the rooms, there was a micro kitchen and a bed and a tube went from the tree to the room. The mice could press a button on the wall to get some water. The mice had a lot of dirt and seeds and lights that could stay on forever so they could withstand a siege. They had a watchtower to know who was there.

At the top of each tree, there was another secret knot door and a glass tube that went from tree house to tree house so that the mice could go from one tree house to the other without touching the ground.

In the branches of the trees, there was a small glass watchout that was completely hidden so that when people were coming, the five little mice could know who the guest was before unlocking the door.

One day, a cat came along. He tried to get the five little mice, but they were safe in the tree houses. So the cat went and made a shelter so he would be able to stay longer. Every day the cat watched to see if a mouse came down out of the tree, but the mice never came down. They did not have to because of the water and dirt and seeds and lights. So, the cat was very disappointed and frustrated.

The cat decided to make a ladder up. But there still was not a way to get in because there were no openings up there! So the cat was very unnnnnnnnnnnnnnnnnnnnnnnhapppppppppppppppppppppppppppppppy.

The five little mice were bothered by not being able to go down so the five little mice said to the cat, "When you will stop chasing us? You know you cannot get in."

The cat started yelling and crying and said, "Right. I will search for other mice or a mouse."

When the cat went away, the five little mice decided to build a boxing arrow detonator on each of their doors because they were really angry that the cat was always sneak attacking them!

In the meanwhile, the cat secretly crawled back up to the five little mice's tree houses so that he might be able to sneak-attack them. But he didn't see the detonators.

The cat pretended to be a mouse and said, "May I come in? I escaped the cat."

But one mouse went up into the watchtower and found that it was the cat. The mouse said, "You are the cat. Go away" and pressed the button on the detonator... ... Suddenly, an arrow shot into the cat's tail.

The cat screamed, "Ouch, what is that?"

Then a few seconds later, the cat lay down on the ground and pretended to be dead until the five little mice went out.

CHAPTER TWO

The five little mice were in one of the five tree houses and they were talking. They were so busy that they forgot about the cat.

The five little mice decided to design an auto playground. They decided to design a monorail that lava appears under. You start falling, and then the lava turns into water. The monorail turns into a boat, but the water disappears. Right after that, the monorail turns into a glider.

The monorail glides up a lot and the wings collapse. Then the monorail falls down until just a few feet above the ground. Then the wings immediately pop out, and the monorail glides all the way back up. This defies gravity.

While the mice were designing, the cat got up from the ground, went into his shelter and went to sleep.

After a while, the cat got up from his bed and went out.

The cat recorded a spooky sound and placed his recorder in the five little mice's main tree house.

At night, the five little mice heard spoooooooooooooooooooooo oooooooooky sounds so they ran around in circles because they were reallllllllllllllllly frightened until one of the mice said, "Wait! The cat made this recording. He must not have died."

So the five little mice stopped running and they went to bed because they knew the cat would not be able to get in.

In the meanwhile, the cat said "Ha, ha, ha! Now I scared the five little mice out of their heads. Ha, ha, ha!"

When the five little mice got up, they immediately started to look for the cat. But they could not find the cat, so they went back to bed.

In the morning, the five little mice started to build a little bit of the auto playground. They built a flinger and a monorail and a person detector. When the cat went into the monorail, the person detector activated the flinger and the cat got flung up and luckily for him he ended up on a cloud. So, the cat made a ladder made out of cloud and climbed down.

Then the cat had an idea. His idea was to go into the tree houses and trap the five little mice. So he made an auto building prison right in front of the door of each tree house.

When the five little mice came out their doors, they got trapped in the prisons. And they were very surprised! Then the cat pulled the prisons into his house. While they were being pulled, the five little mice said, "Just dig under the prisons!"

So the five little mice dug and dug until they were under the five little tree houses. They dug a tunnel up into the tree houses, then they crawled back to the prisons because otherwise the cat would see that they were not there.

After a while, the cat opened the prison doors because he thought, "These five little mice are so smart. Maybe making friends with them will help me." So he said to the five little mice, "Could I make friends with you?"

The five little mice said, "Okay but no killing."

The mice kept building the auto playground for people, and they earned lots of money. They took one man as their student. When the man retired, he had 72 billion dollars. His name was Bill Gates. And that was why there is so much money today. When the five little mice died, the money got distributed.

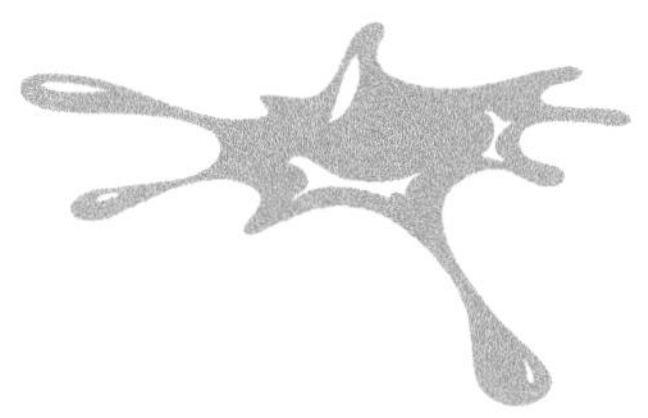

82

Character Details

Frances Lee Hall mentored Timothy Leung through a revision focused on using character details to clarify his characters' feelings, actions, and reactions throughout the story, "The Dragon Journey."

Dear Reader,

In Timothy Leung's tale, "The Dragon Journey," we're taken on a magical adventure led by Clayton, and his quest to find his dragon friend, Thor, a new home.

There is much to love in this story. Clayton's conflicted desires to obey his father while also helping Thor feels real. As does Clayton's resentment over his big brother's ability to hunt dragons. And Clayton and Thor's friendship warms the heart. We can all relate to these feelings. And that is the gem of writing—to allow readers to feel what your characters feels. An editor once told me, "I don't care what your character feels, I care about what your readers feel." Meaning, we as readers don't want to be told what to feel, we want to feel it on our own.

Our revision focus was on character details. I encouraged Timothy to slow down and focus on details, the meaningful descriptions and actions that help make Clayton and his dragons feel unique, and reveal who they are. Character details not only show us what a character looks like, they show us how characters act and react to situations, which in turn, moves the plot along. I was curious whether Timothy's dragons were like Chinese dragons, or something entirely different.

Timothy got to work and created a dragon community that we could imagine in our minds; such as Thor, the baby dragon who acted "like a puppy begging for food… its floppy tongue wagging side to side." Timothy said he read books for word choice ideas, which is an excellent exercise for writers of all levels: combing books for inspiration and being able to read like a writer.

We also worked on the story's climax, or the moment at which the biggest struggle is realized or resolved. In Timothy's original manuscript, Clayton was

determined to convince the villagers to see the dragons in a new light. He succeeded, but this very important moment felt much too quick and easy. Inspired by Clayton and Thor's character details, Timothy created a stronger pivotal moment, which felt more earned and satisfying.

Character details allow readers to get to know characters in deep and memorable ways. Take the time to get to know your characters, by their appearance, by their actions and reactions, and by what they hold most dear in their hearts.

Happy Writing,
Frances

Frances Lee Hall

Inspired by her Chinese American upbringing and family history, Frances Lee Hall writes stories as a way to preserve, share, explore, and honor her Asian American heritage. She received an MFA in Writing for Children and Young Adults while attending Vermont College of Fine Arts. She writes children's book reviews for Kirkus Reviews, blogs on her website and for ReaderkidZ, and lectures about her writing process for schools and senior centers. As a television features writer, she wrote about artists and technology and has earned three Emmy Awards as writer and producer.

Timothy Leung

Timothy Leung is in second grade and lives in Saratoga, CA, with his parents and older brother. He likes to put on magic shows and perform with puppets. As a Cub Scout, he travels on outings and learns new skills, such as using drills and hammers. One of his favorite family vacations was a trip to Las Vegas and the Grand Canyon.

Here are some of Timothy's thoughts on the writing and revision of "The Dragon Journey."

Why did you decide to write a story about dragons?
At first I was going to write a different story. But I like description in writing, and I thought dragons were easy to describe. Then, the dragons could have lots of feelings in the story. So that's why I decided to write a story about dragons.

What is your favorite part about Clayton and Thor's friendship?
My favorite part is when they eat blueberries together, because it starts their friendship and it's a strong event. So they are eating the same things together.

Do you like blueberries?
Yes.

Is that how you got your idea for that?
Kind of!

What was the most challenging part of revising your story?
Picking the right word. It's kind of hard to get the right word that'll give your reader a mind picture.

What did you do to find different words?
I read a book and it had a lot of good words. And I also looked for lists on Google.

Great! Which books did you read that you found helpful?
The Boxcar Children and *The Pilgrim Mystery*.

What do you like most about writing?
As I said before, I like having description because that kind of gives a mind-picture to the reader. And I think the mind-picture is very important.

Why do you think the mind picture is important?
Because then the reader can feel like they're inside the story.

How and where do you like to write?

I like to write in the family room. On my computer.

Do you have another story you'd like to work on?

I'd like to work on other stories, but I haven't come up with them yet.

Are you going to keep writing about Clayton and Thor?

Maybe!

What advice do you have for other writers who don't want to revise their work?

If they don't want to revise their work, then like me, they should add good description. Because as I said, the mind-picture is really important. And the reader would care all about that because they're sometimes lost in the story.

How was your experience, going through the whole Book Contest process of submitting your work, receiving constructive criticism, and following through with revisions?

Since it was my first-time experience, it's pretty cool!

The Dragon Journey

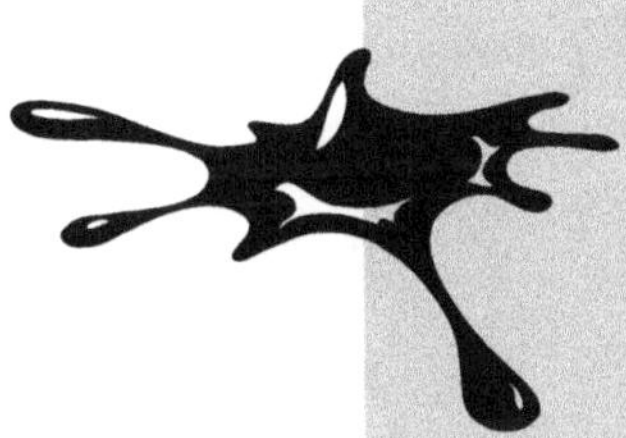

by
Timothy Leung

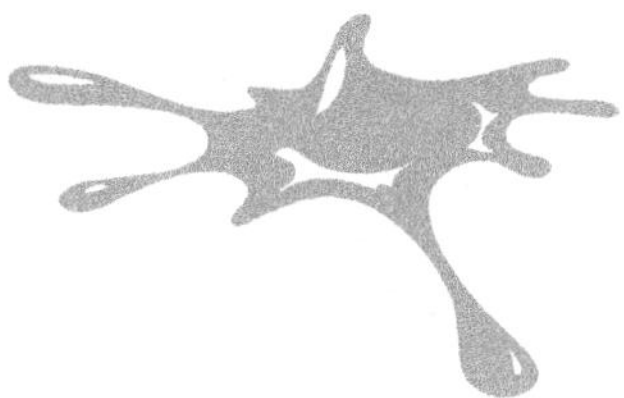

As the sun shone through the bedroom window, Clayton started to awaken in his home. Clayton was a boy with red hair and had plump cheeks with freckles. He was very adventurous, but he still was kind and had a warm heart that made him care about all living things. Clayton's home was very near a village where dragons lived. Many of the townspeople in Clayton's village feared the dragons, especially one in particular. It was the most powerful dragon amongst them all. This dragon did not have a name, so the villagers called it The Powerful Dragon. Since the people in Clayton's village were afraid of dragons, they sent brave hunters to hunt them down.

As Clayton sat up in bed, he heard some cheering outside. The boy jumped out of bed, slapped on a coat, and started to clumsily scramble outside his home while knocking down many pieces of furniture to see what was going on.

"Whoa, whoa, slow down young man!" said Clayton's father to Clayton. "What's going on?"

"There's a huge crowd cheering outside!" exclaimed the boy excitedly. "I want to find out what's happening!"

"Maybe the villagers brought back The Powerful Dragon!" offered Clayton's father, now excited. "But remember, you must always stay with me. Don't touch the dragon and don't go close to it without me."

"Yes, Dad, I know," said Clayton, rolling his eyes and putting his hand on his father's cheek. "You told me about one hundred million times! Let's just check out what's happening alright?"

"Alright," replied Clayton's father.

The two hurried outside the door of their house. *There was good news and bad news*, thought Clayton. The good news was that there was a dragon lying down not looking alive. It was slumped over, with its tongue drooping out and its arms crossed over the dragon's blue, scaly belly. Clayton's mouth fell open in awe and shock. He never had the slightest thought that dragons were this amazing. The dragon had a long, blue tail and a round, oval-shaped mouth with piercing claws and toenails. The bad news was that Clinton, Clayton's annoying *I'm so wonderful* big brother, was proudly inspecting the dragon by pounding on its gigantic tummy and poking its arm. Clinton was slightly taller than Clayton and had blonde hair, plump cheeks and freckles. Clinton was proudly gripping a medal which gave a terrifying signal to Clayton that his brother had killed the amazing dragon himself. Clayton's brother was old enough to go and hunt down dragons. But not Clayton. Clinton would often brag about it. But now, Clayton knew that his big brother would brag about his victorious achievement like he had never had before.

That night, Clayton just couldn't sleep. He was being kept awake for two reasons. The first reason was that Clayton thought that it wasn't fair that his brother got to go on these dragon quests but Clayton couldn't. He knew that it wasn't safe, but Clayton really eagerly needed to go on at least one dragon quest. It seemed so cool, fighting dragons with remarkable weapons. Clayton now was determined to have that beautiful medal that his brother had earned—and the only possibility that Clayton knew was to go on a dragon quest. The other reason that was keeping Clayton awake was that he had the slightest thought that he had heard a whimpering noise.

"Sniffy, sniff, sniff," it went. "Sniffy, sniff, sniffy, sniff."

Clayton wondered what it could possibly be. A raccoon? A dog? Cat? A dragon baby? The thought flashed across Clayton's mind like a shooting star. Clayton thought he could go outside and see what was making this *sniff, sniff* noise. After all, it was bothering him. So why not take a little peek? Alright. Clayton decided that he would take a tiny look. So he quietly crept down the stairs and opened the front door. Outside, Clayton saw nothing.

"Sniffy, sniff, sniffy, sniffy, sniff, sniff," went the noise again. "Sniff, sniff, sniffy, sniff."

Clayton looked at a bush. Nothing there. Clayton looked at a house. Nothing there either. Clayton looked high and low, but still nothing. Just when Clayton was about to give up, he saw a tiny bush rustle. He searched the bush suspiciously, like a detective.

"Sniff, sniff sniffy, sniff," went the noise again.

He ran off and shot a tiny weasel with his bow and arrow. Clayton ran back to where Thor was and handed him the weasel.

"Snuffle?" asked Thor, looking at the weasel curiously.

He took the weasel and immediately started to cover it with dirt.

"No! It's for you to eat!" yelled Clayton.

He stared at the dirt pile that Thor had just made. But when the little boy looked back at his dinner, he saw the tiny baby dragon eating it!

"No, Thor! No!" shouted Clayton.

"Sniffle?" asked the dragon.

"Alright," said Clayton. "If you want blueberries for dinner, then I'll get you some."

So Clayton ran off to pick some blueberries. Thor happily wolfed down the blueberries when the boy brought him more. Soon after the stars appeared, Thor and Clayton fell asleep under the night sky.

The next day, Clayton and Thor were up, feeling as good as new. The two trudged on again through the forest, from dawn to noon. As the time started shifting to afternoon, the two came to three grave looking stones with carved words on them. The middle stone said, *Dragon Valley: Enter If You Dare*. The stone on the right hand side said, *The Dragon Village*. And the left hand side stone said, *You Will Not Survive Here*. Clayton walked past the stones feeling now a bit scared. But Thor was there comforting Clayton by "Sniffle-snuffling."

The two came to a valley. It was a very far drop and Clayton guessed that if any human dared to jump off, they would be injured badly. There were at least one-hundred dragons there. Some were yellow, some were green. Some were purple, but none were blue, so there weren't any Powerful Dragons down there. They didn't have scaly and forked tongues. They had nice round tongues. They were average-sized and they all had wings in a variety of colors. Clayton expected them to be hunting or eating animals, but instead, they were all eating plants, blueberries, and nuts.

Suddenly, there was a loud shriek from the top of a mountain that was looming over the valley. All the dragons looked up as The Powerful Dragon stepped out of a cave and swooped down to the valley. Its broad, blue wings spread out as The Powerful Dragon glided through the evening sky. It had very big feet, but it didn't breathe fire. Clayton expected it to roar, but instead it said, "Garonk! Garonk!"

"Garonk! Garonk! Sniffle! Garonk!" replied the valley of dragons.

Clayton thought it wasn't a very powerful noise. As the valley of dragons did some more chatter, Clayton stared at The Powerful Dragon's cave. It was just a hole in the mountain, with bumpy edges around it. That dragon would be a pretty nice parent for Thor. It would be a pretty nice parent, but it would take a long way to get up to that cave to plop Thor in front of The Powerful Dragon's cave. It looked pretty homey, just fit for a child. The little boy assumed that The Powerful Dragon had children of its own. Clayton decided that he and Thor would climb the mountain at nightfall.

"We're going up there tonight," whispered Clayton to Thor, pointing to the mountain. He didn't want any chance of a dragon hearing the two.

"Sniffle, sniffle," said Thor, nodding.

"Alright then, we are good to go!" said Clayton.

That night, Clayton and Thor crept over to the mountain and

started climbing. Thor was climbing a whole lot faster and better than Clayton. Just when Clayton was about to reach the top, he slipped. Clayton felt himself falling down the giant mountain rapidly... then flying? Thor was slowly levitating up the rest of the mountain, carrying the boy!

"Thanks, buddy!" said Clayton, happily.

When the two got up to the top of the mountain, they were both exhausted. The boy slowly crept into the cave with Thor.

Clayton said, "Okay, buddy, now you'll have a new home here with a new parent to take care of you."

"Sniffle?" asked Thor, leaning onto Clayton's body.

"No, no!" said Clayton, gently peeling Thor off of his chest.

"Sniffle, sniffle, snuffle?" asked Thor again.

"Alright, alright, okay, I'll stay with you a little longer," said Clayton reluctantly. "After all, we both need some sleep."

"Sniffle, snuffle, sniffle," agreed Thor, nodding.

When Clayton woke up, he felt different. He felt as if a huge rock was lying on him. Clayton looked above him. Something was on him, but it wasn't a rock. It was Thor.

"Hey, buddy, cut that out!" shouted Clayton.

"Sniffle!" cried an alarmed Thor.

Clayton peered down the valley of dragons. The dragons weren't sharpening their claws or getting ready for "practice battle." They weren't breathing fire at each other in a fierce way. Instead, they were garonking to each other, in a nice way. They were also playing around. Suddenly, Clayton realized something. These dragons weren't fierce at all! They just fought the humans because the dragons wanted to protect themselves. In the olden days, there were fierce and mighty dragons. So the humans killed all of them. Many dragons had died, but the humans were still scared of the dragons. Thor started licking Clayton. He giggled. Thor licked some more. Clayton at least was happy now.

Suddenly, a loud battle cry pierced through the air. Clayton heard many recognizable voices including his brother's and dad's. Then there were many furious "garonks." Thor perked up in surprise. There was plenty of hubbub and then a few shrieks of terror. Clayton figured out from all the chatter that there was a search party from his village to search for him. The party had bravely traveled to the valley of dragons and had now arrived. All of the warriors came into battle position, ready to fight. Shields had sprang, swords were drawn, bows were being held tight with quivers already on them, and there was plenty of excess armor in store. The villagers were ready to battle the dragons!

Clayton desperately didn't know what to do. He quickly climbed out of the cave and yelled, "STOP!"

"Son!" his father exclaimed, sighing a sigh of relief. "Are you alright?"

"I'm fine!" yelled Clayton.

"Stand back, son," bellowed Clayton's father now in a stern voice. "This could be dangerous. We are going to fight the dragons!"

"No!" yelled Clayton to the villagers. "There is no reason for you to fight the dragons! They are harmless! I saw it with my own eyes!"

"Son!" yelled Clayton's father again. "You shall not disobey me. If you do not get out of the way in ten seconds, you will be punished like never before, and that baby dragon will be burned."

Clayton had never heard his father speak in a tone like this before.

"Bu-u-u" sputtered Clayton.

"Ten…" said his father.

"Father!" begged the boy. "Please, stop!"

"Nine…" continued the father.

"It'll make our lives easier!" tried Clayton.

People started to murmur and agree.

"Eight," yelled Clayton's father.

"Please!" said Clayton. "I am not being hurt up here!"

He quickly grabbed a tiny piece of leftover weasel from his dinner, and a handful of dirt that had been on the cave. He gave the weasel to Thor and sprinkled the dirt in front of Thor. The little dragon buried up the weasel in the bits of dirt.

"Seven," bellowed Clayton's father.

"Don't you see?" asked the boy. "The dragons are harmless! This dragon didn't eat meat, which is the weasel!"

There were loud cheers of chatter and agreement. People were starting to agree with Clayton!

"Six," said his father.

"Please!" yelled Clayton. "How many of you have lost your brothers, husbands, or fathers fighting the dragons?" asked Clayton to the crowd.

He scanned the valley. A wave of hands started to appear from the bottom of dragon valley.

"Don't you see that I am standing up here unharmed?" asked Clayton.

100

People started chanting, "Stop warriors! The dragons are good, not bad! Stop, stop, stop!"

"Five…Four…Three…," said Clayton's father.

Everybody except chief warriors and Clayton's dad were chanting, "STOP! STOP! STOP!"

"Two…, one…, zero!" shouted Clayton's father.

The father shot an arrow directly towards the cave in the mountains. Clayton sprang to one side of the cave, closing his eyes and hugging Thor tightly.

"STOP!" yelled the crowd. The warriors didn't listen. They shot their arrows. Suddenly, Clayton's mother came dashing up the high mountain. When she reached the top, she hugged Clayton tightly.

"Get out of the way, madam!" yelled a warrior. "Let us kill what we all fear!"

Clayton's mother stopped hugging Clayton and looked at the warrior.

"It is not these dragons that I fear," she said. "I fear you, warriors."

The warriors were shocked.

"I have worried too long about my sons," continued Clayton's mother. "You warriors came up and told all men and boys that they should fight dragons! That is dangerous! I could have lost my dear son Clinton on one of his dragon quests!"

Other mothers started emerging from the valley. They climbed up, and one by one they told the warriors on how their sons were killed.

"Whose son wants to be killed by just a sport?" asked Clayton's mother.

"Sport?" repeated the warriors. "You call fighting dragons a sport?"

"Yes, I do," replied Clayton's mother. "It's a sport that you used, to cover the lie. The lie that dragons were evil. They used to be, but you killed them all."

Clayton started to tell the warriors, "You see? Soon, all of the dragons will die extinct! Besides, dragons could mow our lawns and take us flying!"

The warriors whispered to each other about the wise words that were spoken. Finally, they said, "It is true. The boy is chosen trustworthy. Our village will not suffer from the effect of the olden days. These dragons will be helpful for all. Mow a lawn? A dragon comes in. Run an errand? Dragons will take you. This is true. We will always bow to the boy in honor."

The whole crowd cheered.

"And as a present," continued the warriors. "We will let the boy bring home the baby dragon if he wants to."

"Of course I want to!" said Clayton happily. "Of course I want to!"

That night, Clayton was known to all villagers. Clayton looked at Thor.

"Buddy," he said. "I'm glad I chose to take care of you. We wouldn't have discovered the fact that dragons were harmless, right?"

"Sniffle, snuffle," replied Thor.

This time, Clayton thought he understood Thor.

"Good night too," he replied.

And as the stars and the moon grew brighter and brighter, Clayton and Thor fell fast asleep under the night sky.

Streamlining the Plot

Elizabeth Jellison worked with Kabir Aditya Buch on focusing his whole plot so that each event led up to the most important moment, the climax.

Dear Reader,

For this revision, I wanted to focus on building up to the climax, or that moment of the story where the characters have the most to lose.

Everything about this story leads up to the baseball game, whether it is in George's nightmare or in math class, and that is very important. Sometimes, in writing a story, the author can get bogged down in trying to explain everything that happens in the character's lives. But that can make the story drag, so deciding what is necessary to tell the story is an important part of making it flow well for the reader. This is what we spent most of our time on:

First, we thought about the time tables and schedules Kabir added into the story. Were they important for the reader to know for the baseball game? Some of the activities George and Fred do are important for the reader to understand their characters, yes, but is a time table important?

Second, we considered the bit about the missing bat. This part of the story is interesting to the reader, so perhaps developing this section would be more exciting than spending extra time on Fred's dinner or the part of the story when he practiced his tuba. Here are some questions we asked: Why is the bat important? What does it have to do with the final baseball game?

Third, the final game. This is the most important part of the story. Building the tension around this event would make the outcome more exciting, so while reading over it again, we thought about the transition from George's birthday party to the game. How could we make the reader anticipate the game like Fred and George?

Kabir's story is very exciting and a lot of fun to read. I hope you'll enjoy it!

Happy Writing,
Elizabeth

Elizabeth Jellison

grew up in Oregon, surrounded by fir trees, mountains, and fresh air. Much of her inspiration comes from her time spent outdoors as a child, exploring and acting out the fairy princess stories in her head. She graduated from Portland State University with a B.A. in Arts and Letters, and moved to California soon after. She has always loved to write, sing, and perform, and hopes to pass on her passion for stories to children.

Kabir Aditaya Buch

Kabir Aditya Buch, nine, loves reading fiction, and looking up different things on Wikipedia. Once, he knew by heart the first 60 countries in order of size. He has traveled to 25 countries already, but unfortunately, not in order of size. He also likes candy, especially fun-dip. He enjoys playing various sports, including baseball, with his friends at school. The friendly competition is what inspired him to write The Baseball Game.

Here are some of Kabir's thoughts on the writing and revision of "The Baseball Game."

What shifted or changed when you revised your story?
It became more realistic.

Why do you enjoy writing?
Because it's fun.

Where do you like to write?
In the living room using a computer.

How do you come up with ideas for your stories?

I start with characters and how their lives go. Then I think of an event.

Are you working on a new story?

 Yes! I have a character kind of like me.

What is it about?

He gets in trouble a lot.

108

The Baseball Game

by

Kabir Aditya Buch

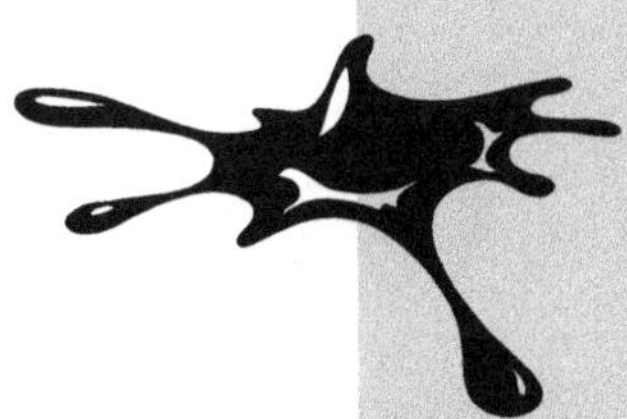

110

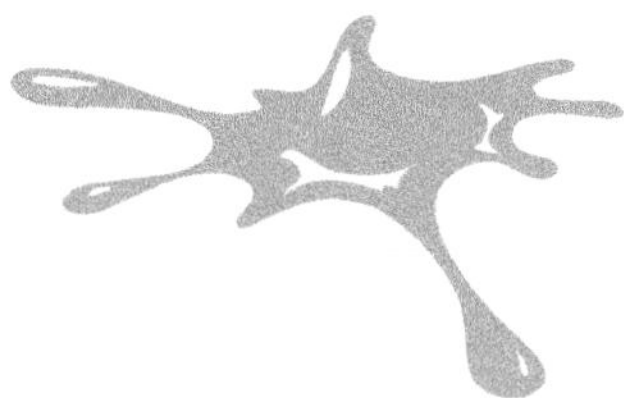

George Xander and Fred Larue, both fifth graders at Nutwiz Elementary School, were best friends. They were even on the same baseball team, The Palo Alto Panthers.

"I can't wait for the Tinfoil Cup Game!" said Fred to George.

The Tinfoil Cup Game was the championship game for their Little League.

"Yeah! Neither can I!" George answered, "But the other team— the San Jose Dragons—they're the best team in the Little League, and you know those three bullies, John, Frank, and Ben? They're on the Dragons!"

When Fred went home, he got out his homework (four homework sheets a day, including Friday, and one per class). Every day, his mom would yell out "Dinner time!" and then, "Freddy (which was Fred's nickname)! Have you finished your homework, showered, and practiced your instruments?"

Mostly Fred would answer yes, but occasionally he would still be practicing his violin and getting ready to practice his tuba, so he would answer no. His dinner time would then be moved to 7:00. This time, he finished quite early, so he got to read his favorite book, *Detective Mark*, about a boy who loves to solve mysteries. Usually waiting at the door for his dad's arrival from work, Fred got so wrapped up in his book that when his dad came home, he didn't even notice, even after his mom yelled, "Freddy, Dad's home!" three times! At dinner, the subject of conversation was Fred's baseball game the following Saturday.

So when Fred's dad asked, "Freddy, do you think you'll win?" Fred wanted to say, "Yup!' or "most likely." Both would've been lies, so he found himself disappointedly saying, "Probably not, because the Dragons are the best team in the Little League."

George's day went very similarly. Unlike Fred, who slept soundly, George had a nightmare that every human and animal wanted to kill him. Even the weapons he was being attacked by moved faster and were not giving him any breathing room, while the unused weapons floated around and acted like somebody invisible was trying to kill him too! Right when he was cornered by lions, leopards, and a few people with guns, George woke up, drenched in sweat. George thought about what had happened in the last few weeks. Since then, he'd had more and more nightmares, and he wondered if this had to do with the upcoming game.

"Hey! George! Fred! Prepare to be crushed!" yelled Frank to George and Fred at Friday lunch recess.

"By whom?" Fred shouted back.

"By us! The San Jose Dragons!" John answered.

"Yeah, we'll put you to your misery!" Ben said.

"Boys, stop yelling." said Mr. Jones, a playground staff member. "And by the way, we're playing baseball on the field."

"You found the bat?" George asked incredulously.

"Yeah, it was stuck in a tree," Mr. Jones replied.

All the boys looked at each other in awe. The bat had been missing since the last Friday, so Fred and George had not been able to get in any practice at school. And why would it be stuck in a tree? John, Ben, George, Fred, and Frank all ran to the field. When they got there, Mr. Jones was already deciding teams. The teams Mr. Jones formed were: Alex, Mitch, Corey, Adam, Richard, Neil, Kyle, Fred, George, and Justin on one team, vs. Ben, Frank, John, Thomas, Max, Larry, Magnus, Alden, Kieran, and Argus on the other. Mr. Jones was always pitcher. He threw to Ben, and Ben batted out of the field, so it was an automatic home run.

"Home run!" Mr. Jones called, "1-0!"

Frank was next to bat. He almost hit it out of the field, but Kyle caught it so it was a pop fly.

Frank swore.

"Frank!" Mr. Jones yelled, even louder than Frank, "Off the field! To the principal's office now!

As Frank stormed off, Mr. Jones said, "Recess is over. It took us some time to find the bat and get it down from the tree, didn't it?"

As the rest of them were leaving, Ben teased George, "We win, you lose, nah nah nah foo foo!"

"That's only because we didn't get to bat!" said Fred.

"What whiners!" Ben replied.

"Yeah!" said John "Whiner, whiner, whiner-whiner-whiners!"

Fred and George walked to math, very frustrated.

Frank was not eager to go to the principal, Mrs. McCartney's, office. He had been there many times and was not sure he wanted another meeting. His meeting with the principal went just as he expected.

"Frank do you know why you're here?" Mrs. McCartney asked.

"Yes," mumbled Frank.

"Mr. Jones told me you swore on the field while playing baseball. Do you think it's okay to swear?"

"No," Frank replied, thinking—though he couldn't believe it—that he'd rather be in math than here!

"Neither do I. Now, why did you do this? I know you are a good kid with a lot of potential, and we want to use that to the best, don't we, Frank Smith?"

"Yes," Frank groaned. He hated this part. It always came up in their "talks."

"I also got a note from Stephanie that you hid the baseball bat that went missing earlier this week, Frank. Is that true?"

Frank absolutely hated Stephanie. She had nothing better to do than spy on people and tell her friends, and if it was bad, tell a teacher too. Half of his trips to the principal's office had been because of her.

"Yes," he answered.

"And why was that? Were you dared, was it a prank, did you want to prevent someone from playing, or was it something else?"

"I wanted to prevent Fred and George from playing," Frank hesitated, his ears turning red.

"Why?"

"Because we're playing a game for the Little League's

trophy, the Tinfoil Cup, and I didn't want Fred and George to get any practice," Frank mumbled.

"I see. But you do realize that this hurts yourself as well as others, not being able to play baseball, don't you?" Miss McCartney said.

"Yes," Frank answered. "I hope you don't do this again, Frank. You are dismissed."

"Okay."

* * *

"Good morning, class!" was how every math class began with Mrs. Parks. Each time, the response Mrs. Parks got was, "Good morning, Mrs. Parks!" in a very bored tone. Fred could only find one reason why she still did this: she thought that perhaps some day all the kids would mature and respond very politely.

"Well, I hope it will never happen again" said Mrs. Parks. "Anyhow, let's get to our problem of the day. George and Fred, whom I will refer to as GF, are in a baseball game against John, Ben, and Frank, called JBF. JBF scores 3 runs every inning except for the 7th, in which they score 1. GF scores 1 run every other inning starting with one in the first. What is the score after nine innings?"

Fred flinched. Could she know about the Panthers vs. Dragons game the next week? Had Mr. Jones told her? George was just as confused. He was not as sharp as Fred, so he didn't get the problem at all. John and Ben didn't really care about the problem. All they noticed was that they were winning, and that's all they wanted to notice. Meanwhile Fred raised his hand.

"Fred?" asked Mrs. Parks, sounding very tired, expecting to be asked permission to use the bathroom.

"25-5," said Fred instead.

"Yes!" said Mrs. Parks, looking very surprised.

Just then Frank walked in.

"Why are you late?" Mrs. Parks questioned.

"I had to go to the principal's office."

"I hope it'll never happen again. Anyway, you missed our problem of the day."

Like I wanted to hear it, Frank thought.

Math flew by, and before Fred and George knew it, the end of the day had come and it was time to go home.

When Saturday came, George woke up to a pleasant feeling. It was March 16th, his birthday, and he was turning 11! When he went in to the living room, there was a stack of presents waiting for him. As he opened them one by one, he found that there were eight presents from his parents and his sister Lucy, which consisted of two Legos sets, three books, and three board games. Then he remembered something that it was his birthday party that evening!

After breakfast, George decided to check out one of his books, *Detective Mark and the Case of the Diamond Knife, #3*. He and Fred even liked the same books! George got lost in the interesting story and his mom had to yell, "George, it's time for baseball!" two times before he heard her voice echoing through the hall. Later, at baseball practice, Coach Lowes was teaching them many new tactics, when he was interrupted by Peter.

"It won't matter anyway, since we're playing against the

Dragons," Peter grumbled.

There was an outburst of murmuring from the team.

"If this is such a waste of time, do you want me to stop coaching?" asked Coach.

Everybody shook their heads.

"Well, you're acting like it. I want positive behavior," he said.

Then Coach Lowes went back to the drills.

George's birthday, at Laser Gun Zap, a place where you have laser guns and you shoot everybody, was very fun. With 1,123 points, George got the highest score of 35 players.

Over the next week, Fred was so nervous that when George brought up the topic of the big game, Fred completely ignored him. He also found himself walking into the fourth grade math teacher, Mr. Johnson's room instead of Mrs. Parks' room. On the other hand, George wasn't nervous at all. He just hoped they'd win on Saturday.

"We have our teams competing for the Tinfoil Cup, The San Jose Dragons vs. The Palo Alto Panthers!" the announcer's voice boomed over the stadium on a clear sunny, day in San Jose.

The crowd cheered. Fred was extremely nervous. There were 500 parents and kids watching this game!

"The Dragons are the home team, so the Panthers will be starting!" continued the announcer.

Fred lined up with his teammates.

"I want our guys batting in this order: Fred, Jack, Peter, Ryder, Kyle, Jim, Andrew, Parker, and lastly, George," said Coach.

"And our teams are on the field!" yelled the announcer. "We have on the Panthers: Andrew, Fred, George, Jack, Jim, Kyle, Parker, Peter, and Ryder! And for the Dragons: Ben, Carl, Colin, Frank, John, Ken, Nolan, Richard, and Will!"

The game started and as Fred stepped up to bat, he still couldn't get used to the fact that this was actually game time, and it was the final game for the Tinfoil Cup. The Palo Alto Panthers' had never made it beyond the quarter-finals! Fred stepped up to the plate. The pitcher seemed to be John, while the catcher appeared to be Frank. John threw. Fred hit it way into the outfield! First, second, safe at third! As he was running, Fred realized that the announcer was only describing the beginning and ending of the games. There was no commentary in the actual game, which was good for Fred, because he preferred no distractions.

John threw to Jack next, and he also hit it into the outfield! Jack got to second base, while Fred ran to home! The scoreboard flashed. From HOME-0 GUEST-0, it now said HOME-0 GUEST-1. When Fred ran back to his teammates, he got a lot of whooping and cheering. Alex batted next, and as he swung, he almost hit the ball out of the stadium, but it was a pop fly. Jack ran to third, but was out by a double-play. There was one out to go, and Peter stepped up to the plate, ready for the pitch. He swung.

"Strike one!" called the umpire.

Peter swung again. The ball flew into the bleachers. It was a home run! The scoreboard read 0-2 now. Ryder was on the plate with the bat in hand. John threw.

"Strike one!" the umpire called again. Strike two and strike three followed.

"Wooooo hoooooo!" cried the Dragons together.

"What braggarts, it's just a strike-out," Fred muttered.

The rest of his team agreed with him.

"Still, two runs is good!" George pointed out, trying to be optimistic.

The Panthers fielding lineup was: Ryder first base, Fred second, Kyle third, George pitching, Peter catcher, Jim shortstop, Andrew, Parker, and Jack outfield. John was up to bat. George threw a fastball, but John hit it, and it was caught by Parker.

"Pop fly!" called the umpire.

Next was Ben. He got a curve ball, and made the mistake of swinging, causing him to hear "Strike one!"

Ben swung at the slider George threw, and Ben hit it. He ran to first, and ... safe at second! The Dragons cheered. Next to the plate was Frank. He hit on his first try. Jack, in the outfield, scrambled for the ball, threw it to Ryder who got Frank out, then threw it to Kyle who got Ben out. It was a double play! The rest of the game went similarly, but at the end of the game, it was Panthers 5, Dragons 4.

"That ends our game of the Palo Alto Panthers vs. San Jose Dragons, with the Panthers winning!"

It sounded like even the announcer was rooting for them, George thought. The Panthers cheered and screamed, while the Dragons booed and yelled, but it didn't matter however loud the Dragons shouted, or how much they screamed, because the game was over. Fred was jumping for joy when a sound over the loudspeaker startled him.

It was the announcer saying, "It seems the umpire counted wrong. The score is really Palo Alto 5, San Jose 5."

Suddenly the tables turned. The Dragons were yelling and

whooping, while George and his teammates sat with gloomy expressions. As the extra innings began, San Jose was playing better, most likely because they had been saved from a loss. But the Panthers were also playing well, for a different reason. They were infuriated. They needed that Tinfoil Cup!

When they fielded, they played like a machine! John hit a would-have-been home run, but Ryder, who was playing outfield, caught it at the warning track. But that wasn't all. He threw it to Kyle, third base for a double play, and got Frank out. San Jose had only one out left, but they made good use of it. Colin stepped up to the plate, and hit a homer! But the run didn't matter. It turned out that the Panthers' offense was even better than its defense! George was batting first. On the first swing, he hit a triple! Fred went up next. And with all his team cheering, he hit an inside-the-park home run!

Fred sprinted along the bases just a few feet away from George. He slid into to home milliseconds before a throw to the catcher was made. At the end of the game, the Panthers were once again cheering, but this time, the win was for real.

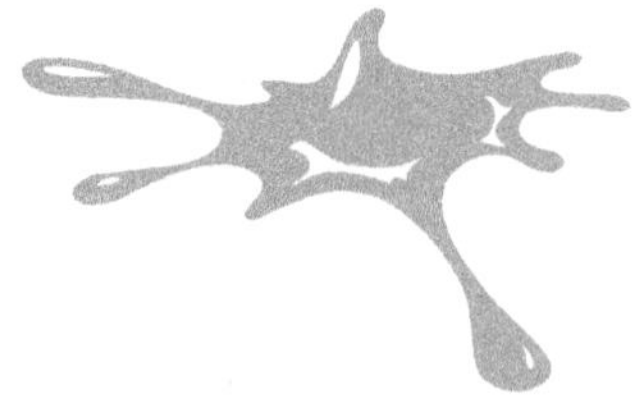

Sensory Detail

risti Wright mentored Olivia Cisneros through a revision focused on bringing the reader into a character's world through sensory detail.

Dear Reader:

With Olivia Cisneros' charming adventure about a lonely cat in Paris who turns new friends into family, we decided to focus on sensory detail to make her Paris setting shine.

Sensory detail includes sight, sound, touch, smell and taste. When it comes to an iconic place such as Paris, it is even more important to use sensory detail so that the reader has the strong belief that she has literally fallen off the pages onto the streets of Paris.

Here are three steps that you can take in order to add more sensory detail into your story.

First, list as many things as you can think of when it comes to your setting that have to do with one of the five senses. Don't limit yourself. Olivia came up with sights such as the Eiffel Tower and the Louvre and sounds such as sirens of police cars and people having conversations at corner cafes. She had her cat smell crepes and croissants and taste tuna and milk. All of these fun details made Paris come alive.

Second, consider where you might put these details into the story. Does your story require some added action or setting description in order to make it possible to add a particular scent or touch or sound? Go through your manuscript and mark all the places where you think you could add sensory detail. Then go through again and actually make the changes. Don't edit yourself too much. You want people to fall in love with your setting as much as they might fall in love with your characters.

Third, read your story out loud. Really! Where have you added too much sensory detail? This is when you do the reality check about whether your setting has

now overwhelmed the story. Keep what you absolutely love and trim the description that's just okay.

Think of your rewrite with a focus on sensory detail as adding frosting to a yummy cupcake. The cupcake is fantastic on its own, but with the frosting it becomes amazing!

Warm regards,
Kristi Wright

Kristi Wright is the author of the middle grade, futuristic *Basker Twins in the 31st Century* series. She writes both middle grade and young adult, and in addition to futuristic novels, she loves to write stories with elements of fantasy or magic. She conducts writers' workshops at elementary and middle schools with a focus on students writing with all five senses and a strong character point of view. A Young Inklings teacher and mentor, she lives and writes in Santa Clara, California.

Olivia Cisneros

Olivia Cisneros is twelve years old and heading into seventh grade. She's a music enthusiast who plays the violin, piano and clarinet. She also takes dance classes and enjoys sports, with her favorites being basketball and volleyball. If Olivia could visit anywhere in the world, her first stop would be Paris, France, followed quickly by Rome and Venice. She loves to read, especially the *Divergent* Series by Veronica Roth, *Wonder* by R. J. Palacio and *The Giver* by Lois Lowry. Olivia lives in Oglesby, Illinois with her parents and sister as well as Musette, the cockapoo, and Jasmine, the cat.

Here are some of Olivia's thoughts on the writing and revision of "A Cat in Paris."

What gave you the idea for "A Cat In Paris"?

I really like Paris. I've liked it for a while. I don't really know how I got the idea of using a cat as my main character, but I wanted the setting of Paris, and I thought it would be cool to do a story about an animal. Most of my stories have been about people.

How was it revising "A Cat In Paris" with adding sensory detail as a revision goal?

Pretty good. After our meeting, I had all the ideas so I

didn't have to think really hard, and rewriting was pretty fun. I think the changes added to the story. I like reading stories that have more detail so I can get a picture of how it is. I think the story is better than it was before I started the revision process.

What did you like and dislike about the revision process?
I liked getting to go back through and fix things that I did wrong. I liked correcting the story and learning ways to add more detail. I didn't have a lot of problems with revising the story. The sensory detail focus didn't change my story too much. Maybe if it had been a more difficult change then that would have made the experience less fun for me, but I'm fine with doing things that will make my story better.

What advice do you have for other Inklings who don't like revision very much?
Even if you really don't want to revise, it's going to make your story better, so I would recommend it even if you don't like it. Maybe the idea of being able to improve a story will motivate people.

When did you start writing?
When I was little I would write little poems for fun. Then I signed up for a Young Inklings class in the beginning of 4th grade, and I got into writing bigger and better stories.

Why do you enjoy writing?
I like that no stories are the same, and it's kind of cool to see how all

different authors have different theories or ideas about things. Even if they do write about the same topic, they're usually pretty different.

How do you come up with your ideas?

Usually the ideas just pop into my head randomly, or they are based on something I've seen or heard. Maybe I just want to use a piece of a scene or a character as a starting point.

Are you working on a new story?

I just started one for Young Inklings. We're all writing mysteries. Mine's about a mystery that happened in the past. This girl finds a diary that was from this other girl in the past. She has to figure out what happened.

A Cat in Paris

by

Olivia Cisneros

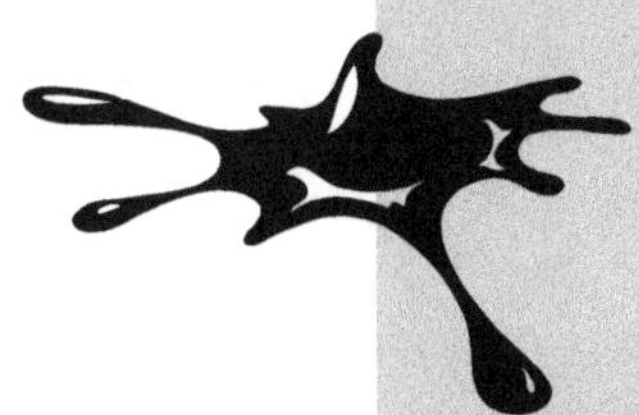

128

CHAPTER ONE

It all started while I was drinking milk waiting for Maman to kiss me good night. She did this every night before she went to bed. A few moments later, she kissed me on my head and walked into her bedroom. I peeked through the small crack left open from the door to make sure she was asleep. I pushed the door open and ran over to the windowsill in the corner of the room. I jumped up and leaned against a pillow Maman had as decoration. After I got comfortable, I looked out of the window into the busy, bright-lit town. Wow! How beautiful did it look from a distance, let alone in reality! In the distance, I saw a triangle-shaped building with glass windows from top to bottom, the Louvre. I leapt down and ran over to my cushiony bed and went to sleep, dreaming about a night on the town, in Paris!

The next day Maman had to run some errands, so I was home

alone, as usual. As soon as I finished my breakfast of protein meat and water, I went over to the sliding glass door and looked through the glass. She has a little kitty door, just for me. I pushed it open and went outside. I felt the breeze brush up against my fur and I suddenly got shivers. I hopped up onto a little chair Maman keeps outside for decoration. I looked around at both sides of the apartment building. I jumped onto the railing of the balcony. It must have rained last night because there was dew all over the railing. It was slippery, very slippery. There was a pipe running down from the top of the apartment building to the ground.

I looked down the pipe, and I swear I heard some noises. I scooted a little closer to get a better look. Then all of a sudden, I slipped on the slick railing and fell straight into that pipe. I was speeding down at least fifty miles an hour!

CHAPTER TWO

"I am going to die!" I shouted sliding downward.

Does this thing ever end? I thought to myself.

Well, wherever I was going, it sure didn't smell the greatest. The pipe smelled like mold and mildew, yuck!

Then I started thinking, *What if Maman gets home and I'm not there? What will she think, what will she do? Oh, I need to get back to that balcony right now and go lie down in my own cozy, cushiony bed.*

I attempted to get back up, but it didn't work. "Uh! It's not working no matter how hard I try!" I screeched with anger. "I give up," I said and simply let the movement of the pipe

130

do all the work.

Then all of a sudden, thump! I fell head first onto the hard ground.

"Ouch, that hurt!" I said under my breath.

I quickly got back up onto my paws and started grooming myself. I looked around acting as if nothing had happened.

"Looks like we got a new visitor," I heard somebody say out of the blue. I quickly shot my head over to the direction in which the comment had come from.

"Who are you?" he asked.

"I'm Rose, who are you?" I asked the strange creature.

"I'm Charlie," the thing said. He was a dirty white-colored creature with brown spots. You could tell he had not eaten in a while, because he was all skinny and scrawny. He was so tall; he was almost two times my size!

"What exactly are you?" I asked him.

"I'm a dog… ever heard of one?"

"Um… I don't think so," I replied.

Charlie told me more about himself and his species while I was having some cooked beef.

"What is this place?" I asked curiously.

"This place is called Sit 'n Stay Café. It's one of the most famous cafés for stray animals in all of Paris."

"Wait… you're a stray?" I asked Charlie as I scooted away from him a little bit.

I wasn't trying to be rude, but I'd heard that strays weren't good to hang around with. It might have just been a rumor, but I didn't want to take any chances. You know, since I come from the rich part of town I'm used to the fancy, snooty, and clean kind of animals.

CHAPTER THREE

So, I ended up talking to Charlie a little more, and he told me how to get back up to my apartment.

"I'll walk you home. I have to go over to that area anyway."

"Okay," I replied as we started walking back. Charlie told me more about himself and about how he became a stray.

"So, whatever happened to your parents?" I asked curiously.

Then, all of a sudden Charlie looked behind him. There was a big, old, white van following us. Then, a guy jumped out and started chasing us.

"Quickly…" Charlie said, "keep running straight until I say to stop."

I was in awe; I didn't even know what to say… so I just ran. I was really out of breath, but I was so scared I kept running.

"What does that man want?" I asked Charlie.

"He's an animal catcher, he takes stray animals to this place… and it's not safe."

"But I'm not a stray," I whined.

"Well he doesn't know that so just keep running."

The air became a cluster of good smelling foods, crepes and croissants! And all I could hear was the sirens of police cars, and people having conversations at corner cafes.

After what felt like forever, Charlie finally said, "Stop."

"Where are we?" I asked, because wherever we were it sure didn't look like Paris. It almost looked like a desert but, not quite.

"I don't know…"

"***WHAT!?!*** What do you mean you don't know," I practically had steam coming out of my ears.

"We must have run too far and got lost. No biggie. Paris wasn't really my style anyway."

"***NO BIGGIE!!***" I screeched "Well it is a biggie for me… in fact it's a huge biggie for me! I have a mother, you know."

"Yeah, yeah, I know I know, you've said that about fifty times already," he mumbled. "If you really wanna get home then we'll find our way home."

"No," I said. "You'll find our way home."

CHAPTER FOUR

So, we started backtracking our route, but we didn't get any closer. In fact, I think we went farther away from Paris.

"Slow down," I shouted.

When I finally caught up with Charlie, I told him that we needed to make a plan.

"Okay, so we need to go to the nearest animal hang out and ask them how to get back to Paris."

So, we started walking. After a while, we finally found an animal hang-out. It was called Paws Up. I thought the name was a little tacky, but the food was excellent! I had some tuna and milk, my favorite.

Charlie got a milk bone with some ice cold water.

We discussed our trip home with this very friendly cat, named June. She was an almost ginger colored cat with brownish blackish stripes, like a tiger. Unlike me who was black with a few misplaced spots of white here and there.

"Well, you are in the small country town of Centre," she said. "It's about one hundred miles away from Paris."

"Whoa," Charlie and I said.

We ran over one hundred miles to get away from an old, shabby, white van? That's crazy; once he saw my collar he would know that I have an owner. Well Charlie, I don't know what they would do to poor ole Charlie.

After we finished eating, we thanked June for helping us and we started walking home. June had also sketched us out a map so we knew which way to go. I liked June; even though I just met her, I felt that I had known her forever. Same thing with Charlie, I just met him, but I kind of felt like Charlie was my brother. He was so much nicer than I could have imagined. Maybe Charlie wasn't as bad as I thought he was. Maybe that saying about strays was just wrong. I then suddenly turned around, and started running back to the hang out.

"Wait, what are you doing?" Charlie asked and started running after me.

CHAPTER FIVE

"June!" I shouted as I pushed the doors open. "June I know we just met, but would you like to come back to Paris with us?"

"Why yes, I would love to go to Paris. In fact, I've always wanted to go to Paris," June replied.

"Well, then what are we waiting for? Let's go back to Paris!"

Charlie, June, and I started running back to Paris.

Oh, did I miss Maman so bad. I wish I could explain what had happened, why I was bringing a cat and dog back home. But I couldn't. I was only a cat, and I can only communicate with animals. And that was the first time I ever realized it. I always treated myself like a human, like I was better than everyone else. But that's when I realized I wasn't better than anyone else; I was equal to any other animal.

Before I knew it, we were already back in Paris.

"Wow," June said. "This is the most beautiful sight I've ever seen."

And she was right; we were standing right in front of the Eiffel Tower! It was surely beautiful. All the detail in the iron work, the multi-colored changing from red, to blue, to pink! Although the scenery was so beautiful, we just had to go back to the apartment, I missed Maman so much.

"Let's go!" I shouted, running full speed ahead. When we finally got back to the apartment, we were all out of breath, but I couldn't stop running. I couldn't wait to see Maman.

When June, Charlie, and I got to the front doors of the apartment we nudged each one open and walked in. We ran up the steps to the third floor. I went to the door which read 4231, which is our apartment number, and pushed the door open. Oh! When I saw Maman, my heart skipped a beat. I felt like I hadn't seen her in so long.

"Oh Rose, where were you? And who are your little friends?"

I think she realized from the look in my eyes that they were strays. But instead of kicking them out, she did the nicest thing ever and kept them. Oh, it was one of the best moments in my life.

So, that's how I ended up with a brother and a sister. Ever since, June and Charlie have been my siblings, and my life has been amazing. And now, I even think that Charlie likes living in Paris. For the first time in my life I wasn't alone, and I'm thankful for that now.

I love my life the way it is now, and I don't ever want it to change.

Pumping Up the Conflict

Mclinda Cordell mentored Kiera Finlay through a revision focused on how to hook the reader in by heightening the conflict in her story.

Dear Reader,

Kiera's story, "William," had a lot going for it, even in its early draft. William was a great character that you could really root for. He had a good heart, he truly did his best to save the other fish from the fishing nets, and even though he had a lot of work piled on him — and really, a lot of lives depended on how well he broke through all the fishing nets — he still managed to come through.

The conflict (which is our focus) was actually pretty solid the first time around. But there was this awesome battle that William only heard about later.

Now, I don't know about you, but if there's any mayhem or crazy stuff going on, I want a ringside seat. If I'm at school and somebody comes up to me and says, "Oh man, Mindy, you should have seen what happened in Biology! A bunch of grasshoppers swarmed the class and ate our homework!" Then I'm going, Wow! Why do I always miss the fun stuff!

So one of the things I asked Kiera in the critique was to let us see the big battle too. And she did! And it was great! So, the first rule to pumping up the conflict is to let the reader see (through the main character) all the exciting action that's going on.

She also made the conflict more immediate by slipping in a little dialogue among the main characters. Instead of sending a letter (as he did in the first draft), Xavier visited William in person wearing a little purple cloak of seaweed. If you can bring the characters face-to-face, that makes the conflict more immediate, especially if those two characters are at odds with each other.

Another thing that Kiera did (and she came up with this on her own) was to have William solve the problem of the fishing nets. In the previous draft, some

other fish came up with an idea to chase off the fishing nets. But in the new draft, William, who desperately needed a way to save all those fishes, came up with the idea himself. Not only that, but he also fixed things to where everybody had a hand in the solution. In a story, it's essential that the main character come up to the solution for the problem — that's how we see that they have grown and learned in the story. When Kiera fixed up the story this way, the ending felt just right.

So let the reader see all the fun action — have the opposing characters speak face-to-face — and have the main character solve the problem. These are all good ways to pump up the conflict!

All best,
Melinda

Melinda R. Cordell is a small-time chicken wrangler from northwest Missouri. Her book, *Women Heroes of the Civil War*, about the women soldiers, nurses, and spies of that epic war, will be out in July 2016 from Chicago Review Press.

Kiera Finlay

Kiera Finlay is ten years old and attends Castro elementary school in Mountain View, California where she has learned to speak two languages (English and Spanish). Kiera likes to eat Indian curry and wants to be a rock climber when she grows up.

Here are some of Kiera's thoughts on the writing and revision of "William."

How did you come up with the idea for William's story?

Well, I like whales, and I was trying to think of a story that could have a character of a whale. Then, I started to think about what a whale would be doing in the ocean. I thought, *You know, maybe they could be saving the fish from the fishing nets.* Then I came up with the whole thing. Once I knew how the beginning was going to be, I came up with the rest.

You started out with one ending, then after you revised, you came up with a new ending. It's like asking "How do you do magic?" … How did you come up with the new ending?

I thought, *How could there be a way that the fish would get in the net and escape?* Then I was thinking, *How would they know when the net was going to come?* Like maybe they knew in advance, so maybe he (William) could notice patterns.

Did having a deadline help you get the story done?

Maybe a little bit, yeah. I may have gotten it a day after the deadline.

How long you been writing?

Not too long…? I've always written stories! I started when I was in preschool, and I would tell my mom a story and she'd write it down. And I did the Illustory stories. That's where you to draw pictures and write stories. Those are best ideas, too! Because the stuff I came up with when I was a kid was awesome.

What's your favorite part about writing?

I like the parts where you come up with a whole idea and how it's going to work. You think about how the story's going to go, and then I also like the part where – I like writing the beginning and end. Writing the middle is fun, too, but it's … the middle. Yeah, it's like, "Okay I've got this space, how am I going to fill it?!" but really, that's pretty good, because when you have a beginning and end, you can find your way through the middle.

142

William

by

Kiera Finlay

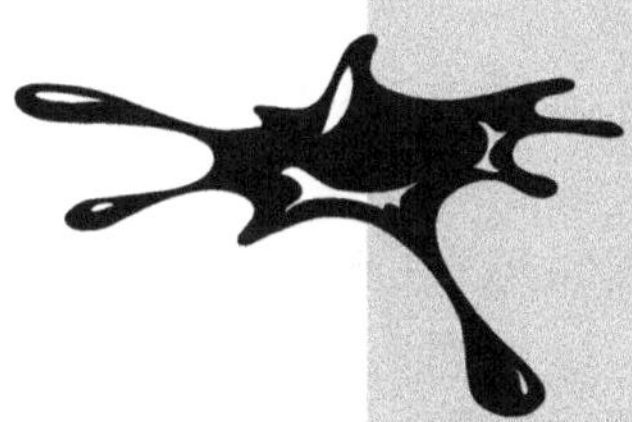

144

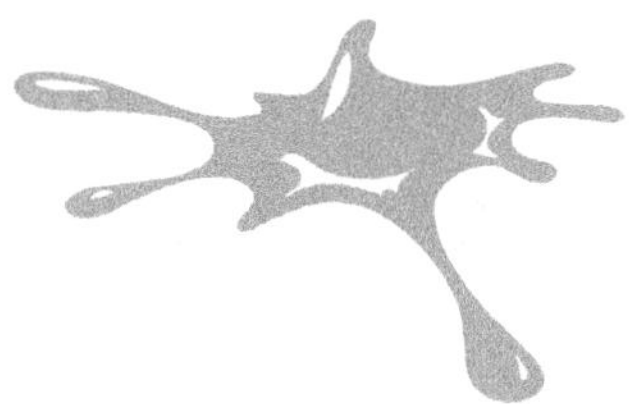

Splash! Rushing toward the sound of a fishing net, I could feel the ocean water pushing against my face. Being a PFNRP (Pacific Fishing Net Rescue Patrol) whale was not easy. I was picked five years after birth by Xavier, a clown fish who is the current leader in the Pacific, to listen for fishing nets all day in an assigned area. Then I (William) was to find the fishing net, and bite it to free all of the tangled creatures. The especially tangled animals were sent straight to Tori, a sea turtle incredibly talented at untangling things. My territory used to be about twenty square miles, but over time it has grown to 100 square miles. This is happening because the numbers of whales is on the decrease.

This is a stressful job and I am not good at doing high pressure tasks. In fact, I am not the kind of whale a sane ocean leader would pick to be a PFNRP. I have no idea what Xavier was thinking when he assigned me this job.

Working like this can be tough, even if you aren't challenged by stressful situations. I do not believe that Xavier should make whales do this work. I have participated in many protests, in hope of getting a new leader. I have only seen him once, when he needed to make sure I could meet the expectations of this job. Most creatures never have seen Xavier.

Today, as I reached the net, I did everything that PFNRP's are supposed to do. I reached the net on time. I delivered a bottlenose dolphin with a rope-tangled snout to Tori. I went back to lying on my listening rock to wait for more nets to come crashing into our wonderful Pacific Ocean.

Only about one or two fishing nets come a day, so I have never had the problem where two come at a time. I have been trained to deal with the first net and then deal with the second, if some day I encounter that situation. I am trained to handle almost any situation you could imagine.

Recently, the PFNRP to my left, Quinn, passed away. I got a letter in the mail saying that I temporarily have double the amount of ocean to cover, until Xavier can find a new whale that fits the job. I was not sure what to think of this, because the PFNRP's always get the blame if they fail to save the creatures caught in the net. Having stress problems, this is a terrible situation to be in.

The next day, I came trembling off of my listening rock (that I also sleep on). Today would be the day I would save at least two, three, or maybe even four fishing nets full of creatures! I asked for help from my mother with the task of listening since I now had a larger area to cover. She would alert me if she heard a net splashing into the water that surrounds our community. My mother was listening for nets in Quinn's old territory, and I stayed upon my listening rock.

That day was very busy. I was wondering the whole time how long it would be until Xavier could find another PFNRP. I saved more fishing nets than expected. I saved FIVE NETS full of sea creatures! That day, I noticed something interesting about the time and location of when the fishing nets showed up. They seemed to repeat the pattern of last Thursday.

Two more days went by about the same as this. Interestingly, the nets seemed to mirror the pattern of the previous week once again. My mother was happy to help both days which I was very impressed by. Spending all waking hours patrolling, though, felt like the exact opposite of a dream job.

The following day I got an unexpected visit from Xavier, who was wearing a cloak of fancy purple seaweed. He was there to tell me that he had noticed my talent in my job, and had decided that I could handle a double-territory by myself permanently.

That was when I almost fainted. Three days had seemed like enough, and now a permanent change? This would not be easy. How much longer would the Pacific suffer Xavier? That night was not one of the best. I could not get rid of the thoughts of unsaved fishing nets and conferences with our leader.

Two torturous days later, news spread of Tori considering trying to get a new leader for the Pacific Ocean. Joy spread through my body, but I still had doubts. How could a sea turtle kick out a powerful ocean ruler? But that very same day I was shocked by Tori herself. While dropping off tangled animals, I asked her how exactly she planned to do this.

She replied, "I've got a whole team with me, and we've got a plan".

The next day, from my listening rock I heard shrieks of surprise and anger, which I figured was most likely Tori battling Xavier.

Later I heard, "Do not destroy our ruler!" which clearly ruined my idea.

I couldn't stay put, so I decided I would try to follow the sounds. Once seeing the battle, I understood. It was incredible being there. Tori's team was capturing Xavier's army first, to weaken him, and would then battle the leader. While watching in astonishment, I noticed the small face of Xavier, almost too small for me to see. He was scurrying away. Tori's team didn't really seem to mind. They knew he wouldn't be coming back. Nobody exactly knows where Xavier went, but rumor had it he was heading for the Panama Canal.

Stories of Tori's victory made its way around our ocean, and I was glad I knew that they were true. Tori is nice, friendly, and generous to all that treat her the same way, and now all can call her a heroine. The next day I checked to see if Tori was untangling animals, and sure enough, she was in her corner working on a puffer fish.

"Wow, you did great!" I said.

"Thanks, it was nothing. He's in the Atlantic now," Tori replied. "But, I never thought of how the creatures are going to be saved, or who could be our new leader."

I thought about all the good creatures I knew, all the animals I had saved, and all of my siblings. Who could be our leader? This was hard.

Suddenly, Tori perked up. "I have an idea!" she said. "YOU could be the Pacific leader!!!"

I was in shock. Just an average challenged PFNRP whale as an ocean leader? Wow. I hoped that was not some of her wishful thinking. Seconds went by as I thought about it.

"We still have a problem though. How will we continue to save all the entangled creatures?" Tori added.

"I have an idea," I said.

"Tell me more!" replied Tori.

Tori and I talked for more than an hour. Tori called a meeting of all of the creatures of the Pacific ocean to be held the following week.

At the meeting, Tori announced: "William is to be our new leader in the Pacific. He has a new plan for saving the tangled animals."

Everyone seemed to be happy with the change, but I can not read minds so I did not know for sure.

After that, I took the conch shell and seaweed microphone and told all of the creatures my plan: "I have noticed a pattern in when and where the fishing nets come. My plan is to watch the fishing nets and send out a letter in the mail to all parts of the Pacific ocean with the fishing net predictions. This will be quite a lot of work, so I need help from willing creatures." The crowd gave a big cheer! Many animals came forward to let me know that they were willing to help.

That was the happiest day of my life. Becoming an ocean leader and stopping PFNRP's in twenty four hours? Incredible. I was overjoyed! I can not explain what I was feeling, but most of all, I felt important. I had just changed many lives and my own. Now that I am hopeful, I can lead a happier life.

150

Building a World

Briana Mitchell mentored Rachel Gould through a revision focused on building the world of "The Little Fairy" by letting the reader in on specific details.

Dear Reader,

When I first read Rachel's story, "The Little Fairy," I was captured by the magical, glittering world she had constructed. What a fascinating world I was drawn into! There were fairies, and mermaids, beautiful landscapes and animals of all kinds. One of my favorite parts about reading stories of the fantasy genre is getting to travel to worlds completely different from our own.

It was clear to me that Rachel has vibrant imagination, and I wanted to work with her to see how real she could make her world. When building a believable world, the devil is really in the details! Every time we spoke, it was clear that Rachel could see every little detail. From the color of each flower all the way to the rules that govern how fairies and mermaids communicate with one another, she had it all down. The trick was working these details into the story so that we, as readers, could feel a part of this new world too!

It was important to look at the rules that made this exciting world tick. We asked questions like: Can fairies and mermaids both swim? Why is it dangerous for fairies to swim? Where do the fairies and mermaids live? Do they both speak the same language? Eat the same food? And on and on the list went!

In the end, Rachel picked the details that were most important to her story, and developed a lovely and captivating world! I'm very proud of her and hope you will enjoy "The Little Fairy."

Happy Writing,
Briana

Briana Mitchell grew up in Portland, OR, where her favorite activities included reading, writing, and running into the forest to act out any freshly woven stories. Since receiving her B.A. in Theatre and Spanish from Santa Clara University, not much has changed! Briana believes that stories are our greatest teachers; and as such, her life was is permeated and shaped by the stories around her. Today, her work as a teacher, writer, and an actor is directly inspired by the power of a well-crafted story. Briana strives to share her passion for the written word with young writers, and empower them to fearlessly delve into the stories they see unfolding in and around them every day.

Rachel Gould

Rachel Gould is a first grader at Almond Elementary School. She's seven and a half, and she was born on November 25th. She's really good at art, and she can draw a picture that looks like a photograph. She really likes to climb trees and she loves reading and writing stories. She can also do a front handspring, a front flip, a back flip and an aerial!

Here are some of Rachel's thoughts on the writing and revision of "The Little Fairy."

What do you think changed about your story?

That she fell in the cave. Because it made more sense that they couldn't find her.

Did you think that much was going to change?

Yeah, I thought it was going to be really hard and I would have to change a lot. And then, when I started writing, I felt like I could do it. I used to be horrible at writing fairy tales, but this story helped me get better at it. I was nervous to write it at first because I thought it would be horrible, but it was awesome!

When did you start writing?

I started writing when I was one and a half. I was jumping around trying to do cartwheels! I could really only write a few words. My brother's three, though, and he can't write yet.

Why do you enjoy writing?

Because it's fun writing and then I get so excited because when I'm finished with my stories I can tell my friends and they like my stories. I never give up on myself and my stories. Even if it's a little weird I won't erase the idea.

How do you come up with your ideas?

Well, I just have to think of anything, like a mouse or a horse or a unicorn. And then you think what you want the story to be about, like who's the main character and what you're going to write about.

Do you like to read? What are some of your favorite books?

I love to read! I'm reading *Henry and the Lost Stone*, and I love it. I have lots of books in my basket, and I've read all of them. I sometimes read chapter books too.

156

The Little Fairy

by

Rachel Gould

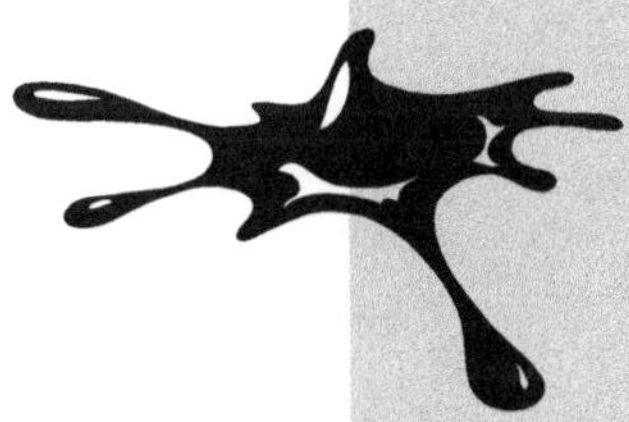

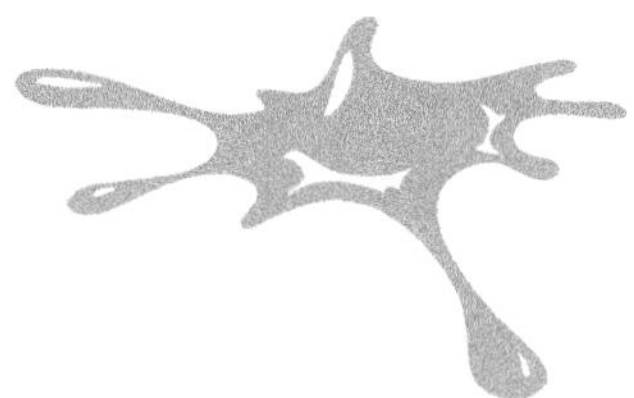

Once upon a time in a far away land where dreams come true, there lived two friends. Their names were Abby and Rosabell. Abby and Rosabell were best friends forever. They never wanted to leave each other. Abby was a mermaid and Rosabell was a fairy.

Rosabell had very, very long blonde hair. Rosabell always wore her hair in a ponytail, and she always wore a reddish pink dress. Rosabell had blue eyes. She also had very light skin. Her lips were bright red. She was very smashing. She lived in the trees with her friends. Like most fairies, she was afraid of everything that was very big. Abby had orange hair and a greenish blue tail, and her top was made of shells. Also, her tail looked like a dolphin tail. Just like Rosabell, she was very beautiful.

Rosabell could speak to the fairies in their language and Abby could speak to other mermaids by whistling. They could also speak English, so they could talk to each other. Abby and Rosabell still had other friends, but they were the best of friends.

One day they wanted to go on a walk, so they got out of their beds, and said, "Let's go for a swim and a fly."

They laughed because it was funny. Abby dove in the water and Rosabell flew above her. They saw beauty around them. They saw butterflies and rabbits. They saw so many birds in the forest.

Soon, the clouds started to get grey. Five minutes later, it started to drizzle. Three minutes later the drizzle was even harder, and then it started to rain. Rosabell couldn't fly and dropped right into the water. She sunk deep down to the bottom and was sucked into a crack. Abby was scared. Abby wanted to save Rosabell. Abby knew she had to get help. But how?

Rosabell held her breath as she fell into the crack. She couldn't hold it for very long and thought that she was going to die until she came up into a cave. The cave was yellow and only half full of water so she could breathe. There were no flowers or food, just water. There were other rocks so she could lie on them. She could not fly still, so she swam to the rocks. It was awfully cold. She was very scared. She was shivering. She hoped that she would see her friends again. She wished that she could at least see Abby.

How can I help Rosabell? Abby thought.

She needed lots and lots of help. Then she remembered if she shook the trees the fairies would come. So she climbed out of the water up onto the rocks that were close to the trees, and she shook them back and forth, back and forth.

Boom boom! When she shook the trees, all of the fairies came out. This was the sign that someone was

missing.

Abby yelled, "Rosabell fell into the water and through a crack!"

Abby started to cry. She said that it was raining and Rosabell fell into the water. All of the fairies were sad but for one fairy who was very mean. Her name was Lavender. All of them cried but the evil one. She just started to leave. Abby yelled at the fairy asking why she was leaving, and the fairy said to not blame her that she was not a part of this. Abby was so mad. She started to whistle. All of the mermaids came to help Abby. Abby told them to get the evil fairy. The other fairies were confused.

This made everybody yell at each other until Abby yelled "Stop! We are wasting time and need to help Rosabell!"

The mermaids and the fairies had an idea. They all said at the exact same time, "We need to get a vine."

"We will help pull the vine, but a fairy needs to go through the crack and to find Rosabell." Abby said.

One of the fairies said that she would do it. But would it help save Rosabell?

"Please get in! Do you want Rosabell to die?" asked Abby.

"No," said the fairy. "I will do it!"

"Yay! Yes, thank you," everyone yelled.

She climbed on. Abby pulled her down until the fairy was at the bottom. She went through the crack. She brought the vine with her. Then she was in the cave. She slowly swam through the cave. She saw Rosabell. Rosabell was crying. She went to her and said, "Rosabell, it's me Lavender!"

Rosabell asked, "How did you get here?"

"Well, Abby and I had an idea, so I said I would come down here into the crack. Then I saw you."

"You found me. How are we going to get out?" Rosabell asked.

"From the vine of course!" Lavender replied. "Oh! I did not see the vine!" Rosabell exclaimed.

Lavender and Rosabell climbed up to the highest rock and grabbed onto the vine. Lavender squeezed her hand through the crack and gave a thumbs up. There was a mermaid waiting there named Waterfall. Waterfall is a mermaid and Abby's friend. When Waterfall saw the thumbs up, she swam up and told Abby that she and the other mermaids could pull up the vine. They pulled Lavender and Rosabell up.

Abby smiled and said, "You are okay!"

Then the two of them swam and flew away together.

Pacing

Laura Schmidt worked with Ashley Schwatka on bringing out the most emotionally engaging moments of her story, "Dance With Me," by focusing on pacing.

Dear Reader,

I was so happy to get the chance to help Ashley with her beautiful story, "Dance With Me." It is a heartfelt tale she's told and I greatly enjoyed working with her.

Editing is an important final step in the writing process. Sometimes, we edit our own work, correcting our spelling (or letting the computer do it) and moving things around. Then, before a story is published in a book or magazine, it goes to an editor. The editor helps the writer see their story with fresh eyes, just like a new reader would see it. We spend so much time with our stories in our minds, it can be hard for us put ourselves in a reader's shoes. That's why editors are so great!

Ashley's revision focused on pacing. Pacing means the speed or pace of the story. The way we tell our stories, which moments get more of our readers' time and thoughts, has a huge effect on how they experience the story. "Dance With Me" was already using a lot of amazing pacing techniques to create a very emotional story. By paring down the beginning, cutting select paragraphs and sentences, we were able to strengthen the tale and make it even better.

Ashley's story is about hope and friendship, even in hard or lonely times. I am so honored to have had the chance to work with this talented young author. I look forward to seeing her stories in the future.

Happy Reading,
Laura

Laura Schmidt is a story-obsessed word-freak who is so excited to join the Young Inklings team this year. She personally thinks that somewhere, all stories are true, and one day she'll open or a door to Narnia or fall into Wonderland. Despite this tendency, she's been granted an MFA in Writing from California Institute of the Arts and BA in Humanities from San Jose State University. When she's not writing or inspiring young minds, Laura enjoys tackling knitting projects she will never finish.

Ashley Schwatka

Ashley is in eighth grade and attends San Jose Christian School. She loves to write stories, whether they be fan fiction or original, and draw. She draws most of the characters that she writes about, and has a passion for animation and digital art. DreamWorks is her role model in life, and when she grows up she wants to be an animator for them. She loves all animals and nature, and enjoys drawing made-up and mythological creatures.

Here are some of Ashley's thoughts on the writing and revision of "Dance With Me."

How did you feel about the revision process?

I was surprised at how much I noticed because of my mentor's comments. Laura would mention something about my story and I'd realize, *Wow that is so true!*

Do you usually do any sort of revision on your own work, on your own?

Not too much. I always read over what I've finished, a chapter or a story, making sure I fix any errors that jump out at me. But not a lot, I don't really edit too much.

How did you get the idea for Milo and Ciela's story?

I was drawing their characters, before I had any story, and I was listening to a song from *Legends of Zelda* called "Song of Storms," and I was listening to that and I pictured them dancing to it, and was just like, I need to write this down!

What is your advice for Inklings who are working on their stories?

I've noticed, because I've written and not finished so many stories, that you really need to find that one topic that you can really do, that you're really excited about.

How long have you been writing?

Oh man, I don't even know. I know I wrote stories in school back in first grade. I think I started writing them on my own a little after that. I was probably about eight years old when I started writing stories for myself.

Drawing is a big part of your story-telling. Do you usually start by drawing characters, or do the stories come first?

It kind of depends. My sketchbook is always filled with random characters, and if I really like them I start thinking about them more and more and start thinking about what their life would be like. But sometimes I get an idea in my head and I have to start writing about it and then as I go I start thinking about what the characters would look like. So…it goes both ways.

What are some of your favorite books?

I have a favorite series called *Wings of Fire*, which is about a dragon war, it's really cool. And, wow, how could I forget *Warriors*, which I just really, really love.

Do you ever get stuck, in your stories or your drawing, and what do you do when you get stuck?

Yes. I definitely get stuck sometimes. I stop for a while, go look at something else, try and get inspired by that. I watch a lot of videos, a lot of animations online. If I really like something that happens, I'll try and think about how my characters might react to that or if that could happen to them.

Who do you usually share your stories with?

My friends and my parents. I like sharing my stories with people.

Do you plan on continuing your writing in the future?

Definitely. I want to keep writing stories and hopefully learn to animate to start to animate my own stories.

Dance with Me

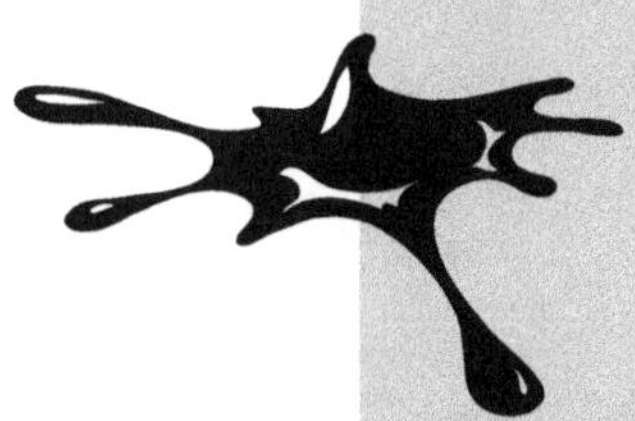

by

Ashley Schwatka

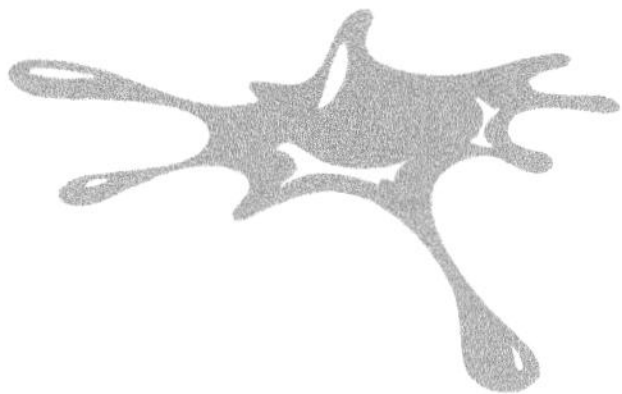

A storm began. Rain fell soft, then harder. Wind blew, brushing the leaves of the trees with grace and elegance. The creatures of the world took cover in their homes, protected from the cold. Nothing moved other than the elements of nature that stood firm, withstanding yet another day of weather. Only the howling wind, whooshing leaves, and cracking rain could be heard.

A furry, light-brown creature sat on the edge of a cliff. It was cat-like in its build, but had much larger ears, a thinner, more pointed muzzle, and a much longer, thinner tail. Two large wings protruded from its back, tucked tightly against the creature's sides to protect their feathers from the tearing wind. Its fur was matted into spikes by the rain, and its claws gripped the grass to steady itself against the storm.

The creature gazed on, over the treetops of the forest below, eyes narrowed to keep out the water. A large gust of wind swept past, catching under the creature's wings and ruffling its feathers into odd positions.

Why it sat here, it didn't quite know. It lived alone as a wanderer, but had just that day found shelter in this area. It could be there, right now, protected from the harsh wind and pounding rain. But for some reason it was drawn to sit here, nearly getting drowned in the storm, even though he had no reason to enjoy the pins and needles pricking at his skin. Milo was his name.

As he thought about it more, he realized that he did know why he was here. He was contemplating. He had just recently witnessed a father save his baby from falling into a raging river. When the father had calmed the baby down, the mother had come running to the sound of crying and scooped the baby into her own wings. The father and mother both smiled in relief and kissed each other. Milo had watched them leave the area soon after, their sides brushing as they walked with their baby. He had been deep in thought for a few days after, thinking about how he was alone, with no one who would ever be with him. That was why Milo was sitting out here in the rain.

And what a fitting environment for being as downcast as he was. He looked out at the sky, filled by sheets of rain. Was he waiting for something? He blinked and watched another leaf fly by. Nothing was here but him and his worries.

Then he saw it. A sleek shape slithered through the air, with two large wings keeping it aloft. It was far away then, but it was getting closer by the second. It made no noise or sudden jerking movements, which left Milo staring at it inquisitively. A flash of lightning lit the sky for a split second, showing a glimpse of blue on the creature. He tilted his head in curiosity, awaiting its further approach, and contemplating a return to his shelter; he wasn't in the mood to do anything social at the moment, therefore if the creature out there wanted to talk to him, he would turn tail.

The figure drew closer, and as it did, Milo prepared himself to get up. It kept pumping those big wings. Yes, it was definitely set on Milo. He looked at his tail on the ground next to him, getting ready to make the walk back into the forest, taking a deep breath before taking what he assumed would be his last glimpse out over the forest for the night.

But as he looked back out, the figure who had been flying his way was right in front of him, making him jump. He was about to make a rude comment about it scaring him out of his fur, but he was captivated by the newcomer. It was quite obviously a female, having long, feathery eyelashes and housing a bit of a bulge on her chest area. Her body was mainly a light aqua blue color, with a white belly and chest and darker blue tail fins and flight feathers. From her forehead to midway down her neck jutted a collection of horn-like spires, the same color as her body. She had no legs but had fin-like hands, and two large ears sat on either side of her horns. Overall, she looked like a majestic, winged seahorse. The most stunning part about her was her eyes. They were bright sapphire blue, and stared into Milo's with a innocent glimmer of curiosity.

A small smile stretched across her pointed snout as she saw Milo's shocked face. To his surprise, she spoke, and with a voice as smooth as silk.

"Why are you out here? Do you like the rain as much as I do?"

Her voice was enchanting. Even over the deafening pounding of the rain he could hear her perfectly, as if they were in a silent, empty room. It captivated him.

Realizing that she had actually asked a question, he snapped out of his trance. "Oh, uh… I don't exactly like the rain, just–"

"Then why sit here and get pounded by it?"

Again he was awed. "I… I don't know. I was just thinking about something…" He trailed off.

She blinked. "Oh. I understand. It is a bit uncomfortable to be in a small space like a den when you have something big on your mind. And what better place to think than in the midst of a storm, right?"

She had read his thoughts. She had just said exactly what he was thinking earlier. "Y-yeah, I guess–"

Before he could say more, she moved from her spot in front of him, circling him once and looking at him from behind. "I could help, you know."

"What do you mean?"

"I could teach you to love the rain. I could take away your worry," she said with a grin.

Milo stepped away from her. "I'm not sure where you're going with this…"

Before he could get too far away from her, she took hold of his paw. "I could teach you to dance with the storm," she explained, floating only a foot or so from him. "I swear, It would take all your angst away. It works for me every time I feel down. Except… it always works better with a partner." She enunciated the last word and her smile grew even more.

"A partner…?"

"Dancing is an art that is meant to be done with a partner, you know."

"Yes, I know that. But… well, I don't really dance. I'm not

exactly the most 'social butterfly' you'll ever meet." Milo's eyes darted to the ground for a split second.

She let go of his paw and beamed quite animatedly. "Well, that's alright! I'm not really, either. I usually spend my time flying by myself. I don't have a flock to be with anymore, since I… Well, heh, that's a story for another time!"

Milo was becoming more interested. "Well…" he tried, "I guess we both have the same kind of story, huh?"

She nodded, her enchanting grin returning. "Ha, I guess so!" She looked out over the forest, just as Milo had been doing when he was alone only a few minutes before. "Hmm. You have a nice view from here."

He followed her gaze, this time actually trying to see it as a "nice view." "Yeah… I guess it is kinda nice, when you look at it right." He shivered again from the freezing rain. "Not really in this weather, though, huh?"

She didn't take her eyes away from the view. "Well, when you learn to appreciate storms, it looks at its best."

There was silence for a while as both of them looked out, one loving what she saw, and the other just trying to. Milo broke the silence first. "What's your name?"

She looked at him and the corner of her mouth turned up. "Ciela. What about you?"

A strange bubbly feeling found its way into his chest and he had to look at the ground. "Milo."

He heard Ciela laugh. "Hey, you smiled! That's the first time I've seen it!"

Milo's eyes widened, surprised. He hadn't even noticed the small grin that had made its way onto his muzzle.

"Ha, I like how your fangs stick out!" she giggled again.

For the first time in months, Milo laughed. "Y-you do…?"

"Yeah! It's cute!"

The surprising and sudden feeling of blush under the fur on his cheeks made him grin even bigger. "Ha! W-well, thanks, I guess."

Silence overcame both of them for a few seconds. Milo wasn't even minding the rain much anymore. This was the first time he'd had an actual conversation with another creature in almost a year. It felt unbelievably good.

Ciela spoke first. "Do you want to dance now?" she asked excitedly. "Now that you are in a better mood, and it seems like you trust me a little more."

Milo looked at the grey sky again, contemplating. "Uh, I don't know. I've never really flown in a storm before. It doesn't seem like a really good idea, to me."

Then he noticed Ciela looking at him with laughter in her eyes and realized that she didn't even have a possibility of landing, in the first place. She had no legs. "I-I mean, for a creature like me," he tried to correct himself. "For you it must be easy, because you have to do it whenever there's a storm, anyway. You must be used to it, right?"

She smiled. "Yes, quite. But just because you haven't done something before doesn't mean you shouldn't try it now!"

He looked at the ground nervously.

"Oh, come on. I promise I won't let anything bad happen to you."

"I don't know… Maybe, I guess, but–"

"Awesome!"

Before he could say another word, she had grabbed his paw again and was suddenly pulling him toward the edge of the cliff. He opened his wings slightly to try to hold himself back.

"Whoa, wait!"

Ciela giggled. "Don't worry! It's super easy!"

"Whoa!"

With that, Milo was shoved off the cliff into the whirling air. Immediately he thrust his wings outward to steady himself, but that only seemed to make things worse. He was held aloft now, but he was swinging out of control. "Hey, C-Ciela! Help me!"

"Don't worry!" he heard her call out. "Just flap with the wind! Push along with it!"

He frantically tried to make the most out of the tiny tidbit of information he had been given, working it around in his mind, trying to make sense out of it. He flapped violently, giant raindrops pounding on his head and back, trying to return to a stable position. *Flap with the wind*, he repeated in his mind. What the heck is that supposed to mean?!

Frantic and scared, he squeezed his eyes shut and called out again. "CIELA!"

At that, he felt her smooth figure fly under him, giving him a boost upward. Shooting his eyes open, he flailed, alarmed, and tried to use that boost to his advantage. Still, he was out of control. Abruptly, she appeared in front of his face. Reaching on both sides of him at once, she fixed his wings to a strange angle, and suddenly he was thrust forward and away from the cliff-side. The wind had caught him in exactly the right way. Was that what she had meant by 'flap with the wind'?

"There you go!" he heard from behind him. "Just like that!"

Intrigued, he tried to remember the angle she had put his wings at and tilted his wings back the same way. He wasn't thrusted this time.

"I don't get it!" he shouted aimlessly.

"Tilt your wings to the wind!"

Right then something clicked in his mind. He had to match his wing angle to make a parachute for the wind to catch on. He focused, trying to find the direction of the wind. He found that when he focused on it, it was quite easy. It had shifted to coming straight from under him. Understandingly, he angled his wings against it and he was thrust upward. He was using the wind to move without barely flapping!

"There you go!" he heard Ciela shout happily. "Get control over it!"

Milo, feeling the pleasure from his success form into a smile on his face, felt the wind shift again and angled his wings back down to follow it. Leaves from the forest swirled up and into the air around him, following the same wind current as him. He watched them with calm eyes. He grinned, not scared anymore, but completely in control. The wind changed again, and he tilted his wings once more. The breeze whistled around his ears, blowing them back and ruffling the long fur behind them. His fur was rain-spattered and matted, but he didn't care. He was deeply focused.

All his senses were homed in on keeping control, and as each second went by, he felt it becoming easier and easier. As another, different gust flowed around him, he noticed it formed a sort of loop. Eager to try the idea that had just popped into his head, he grasped the direction in his senses and latched his wings onto the wisp. Triggering a jolt of adrenaline to burst inside Milo's chest, the wind swept him upside-down, and he made his body streamlined to it. He spiraled around in the storm's grasp, strangely controlled and calm.

As the spiral ended, he was surprised to find Ciela above him. He didn't bother to come right-side up, but instead smiled at her. She blinked and smiled back. With a swift motion, she grabbed his paw and flipped him back over. She flew under him, wings tilted down in an upward glide, and twined her tail with his. He looked down at her, and she beamed up at him.

They were both thinking the same thing: It was wonderful to have someone to enjoy moments like this with.

She brought her head up behind his. "Milo," she whispered in his ear. "Let's go higher."

He smiled and nodded. Ciela moved out a few feet from his side so they could both have room to flap, and Milo pumped his wings to thrust himself upward. Ciela followed close behind and began spiraling around him as they went up. She winked at him, and he got the hint. He began spiraling, too, and suddenly they got the sensation of dancing.

At the same time, they broke the lower layer of clouds, coming into a less windy environment. All around was grey and black, and the rain was more spaced out. The wind that still existed swirled in complex corkscrews and loops, but it was easy now for Milo to stay controlled.

Ciela kept up the pace when she broke the clouds, doing a wide back flip. Milo watched her, never having lost his grin, and flew close to her when she came back up. She laughed gleefully, brushing the underside of his chin with her finned tail. His grin softened as he briefly closed his eyes, enjoying the delicate touch, before opening them again and coming up closer to her. Affectionately, he rubbed his nose against hers, earning a sweet giggle. With that they parted again and twirled around each other.

They continued dancing for what seemed like an eternity.

Soon they began to drop back down below the cloud layer, tails twined. Milo knew it had to be over, but with all his heart, he wished it could go on forever.

When they neared the cliff where their time together had started, Milo slowed himself and landed smoothly on the grass. He turned back to Ciela with a caring smile. She smiled back, looking at him with a beautiful sparkle in her eyes.

"I wish that could have lasted until the end of time," he sighed.

Ciela beamed at him. "We can do it any time you like, Milo. I'll always be out here when it storms. Just call for me and I'll be with you." She glanced to the side, frowning. "Though… I wish it would storm more often… I can only fly in the rain, so I follow this storm wherever it goes. But next time it comes through here…"

Milo brushed her cheek with his wing, getting her to look at him again. "I promise," he said. "I will come here next time it storms. I wouldn't want to miss another dance with you for the world."

She smiled softly. "Yeah…?"

"Yeah."

Her smile grew quickly, and before Milo knew what was happening, she had kissed him softly on the lips. "Thank you, Milo," she said. "Thank you for dancing with me when no one would. I will remember it forever."

Milo's tail curled as he took in her last action.

"No," he said. "Thank you. You helped me so much. You made me happy when I didn't think I ever would be. That I will remember for all of eternity."

Ciela took hold of his paw and gazed lovingly at him. "We both did each other a favor, then." She touched her nose to his paw. "I will see you again, I swear it."

He returned the gesture. "And you, as well."

Hesitantly, she flew out a few feet, then turned back to Milo. "Goodbye," she said in almost a whisper.

Milo smiled reassuringly. "Farewell, Ciela."

With one more smile, she moved out a bit further, and disappeared in a flash of lightning.

Weeks passed before another storm passed through. Milo, just upon hearing the thunder faintly begin, dashed back to that cliff-side, thrilled to be able to meet with the enchanting creature who had pointed his life back upward.

As he reached it, he stopped, heart racing with anticipation. As the rain spattered against his face just as it had that night, he called out her name into the tearing wind. In a flash of lightning, she appeared, her magnificent eyes wide and filled with joy. As the two met each other's gazes once again, Milo spoke the thing she most wanted to hear.

"Dance with me."

Character Motivation

Ann Jacobus mentored Sonia Cherian through a revision focused on strengthening her main character's arc by focusing on motivation in "Goodbye, India."

Dear Reader,

Sonia Cherian's "Goodbye, India" is a story full of the sights, sounds, textures and spicy scents of a village called Thiruvella in India. It's about a girl named Nina who must leave it all behind, as well as her beloved grandmother, to go with her family to her father's new job in England. In an effort to make the move easier on his children, Nina's father doesn't tell them the news until the day before they're scheduled to leave—and about half way through the manuscript.

Sonia does a great job of showing the reader how

much Nina loves her village, her family, and being with her grandmother. We also understand how hard it is for Nina to say goodbye. In revision, we decided to make clearer to the reader what Nina wants, and to make her arc in the story—or how she changes—stronger.

Sonia achieved this by developing and emphasizing what was already there. She revised interactions between the characters as well as internal dialogue in order to bring out both the love between Nina and her Amachy, and to give the reader foreshadowing of the difficult transition ahead. Now, Nina's grandmother tries to soften the news for her granddaughter ahead of time by hinting—also alerting the reader that something is up. Nina then has a chance to think and even worry about it. Later Nina also asks her mother about her family's decision, increasing conflict here (just a little) as well. We see Nina struggle earlier and more with the change she must make, so her motivation and her internal journey or arc, are clearer. It almost always strengthens a story when we make things harder for our characters!

Happy reading, writing, and revising,

Ann

Ann Jacobus earned her MFA in Writing for Children and Young Adults from Vermont College of Fine Arts. She's published short fiction, essays and poetry and her YA thriller, *Romancing the Dark in the City of Light*, will be out from St. Martin's Press in October 2015. She lives in San Francisco with her family.

Sonia Cherian

Sonia Cherian is in fourth grade at Walter Hays elementary. She enjoys reading, writing, and playing with her dog, Leo. Baking is also one of her favorite pastimes, as she likes experimenting with different flavors. When she grows up, she hopes to become a doctor, but write books on the side.

Here are some of Sonia's thoughts on the writing and revision of "Goodbye, India."

What changed for your characters in your revision?

Main character, Nina, feels stronger about staying in India and sadder about leaving. She also now brings leaving up with her mother. Not so much changed for Amachy as she still wants the best for her family, but in this revision, she tries to soften the blow for Nina.

How did you come up with your ideas for the changes?

I tried to pinpoint areas that would work naturally. For example, when they are cooking dosas and Amachy says you could get better ones in England. It was a good place because they were discussing something that Nina knows a lot about. Dosas are very common in India and they make a good symbol of home and what Nina doesn't want to leave.

186

How do you feel the revisions affected your story?

I think that the revisions made my story better. We get to know Nina and her grandmother better. You learn that because Amachy wants what's best for her children, she tries to soften the news ahead of time so Nina maybe won't be so crushed by it.

What advice do you have for other young writers who don't like to revise?

In the end, it's worth it even if you don't like to revise. It helps your story even though it's hard to do.

Are you working on a new story?

Yes. It's about a girl and a phoenix. The girl thinks phoenixes may have something to do with reincarnation, but when she finds one to study, she realizes she might have to harm it and she's not willing to do that.

What are some of your favorite books?

A couple of books that I've enjoyed recently are *The Enchanted Castle* by E. Nesbit and *The Amazing Sea Otter* by Victor B. Scheffer.

188

Goodbye, India

by Sonia Cherian

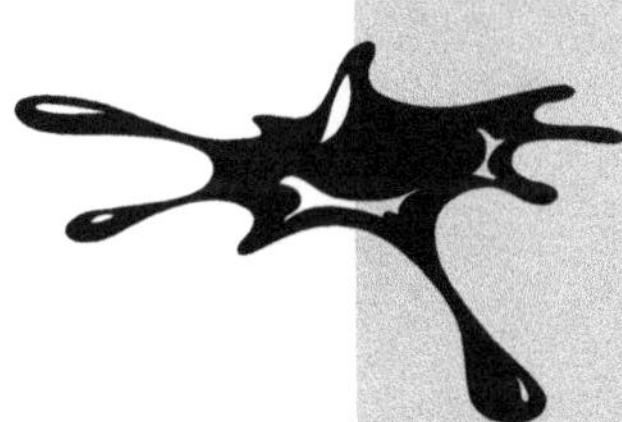

190

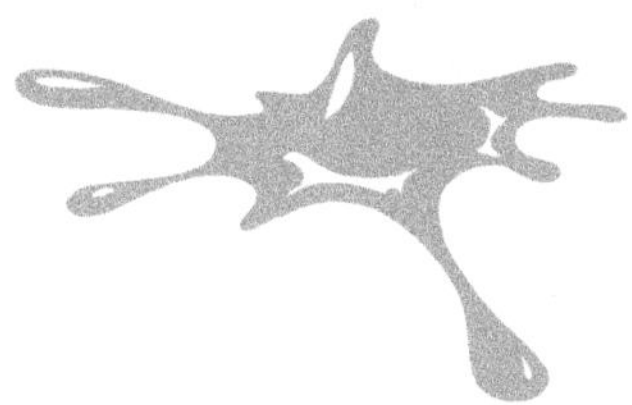

The shrill crow of a rooster jolted my eyes open.

"Nina! If the chickens are awake, then you should be too!" Amachy called merrily.

I flung off the warm, paisley cover and raced to the kitchen, eager to begin the day.

"Good morning," I greeted Amachy.

"Same to you," she replied. "Please get some water from the well, will you?"

I nodded in response and trotted out the door and into the courtyard, inhaling the fresh smells of morning. It did not matter that I was in my pajamas; morning work had to be done.

My bare feet glistened with dew from the damp grass. Amachy's small pet monkey, Mishi, shrieked a hello to me from the jackfruit tree. He thoughtfully licked his hands, sticky from the fruit that he had been feasting on during the early morning.

I finally reached the well. I grabbed hold of a scratchy rope with a pail attached to the end and dunked it into the water. The result was a splash that satisfied me every time I heard it, which was quite often. I nearly fell backwards trying to heave the rope out, as I was only nine and small in size. At last, the rope was up. I undid the knot that attached the rope to the pail and lugged the pail back home, waving goodbye to Mishi.

"I have the water, Amachy!" I exclaimed as I ambled through the door.

"Thank you, Nina," she said, taking the pail from me and emptying it into the large water bin.

"You know," I began, "The jackfruits look ready. May I pick one?"

"That would be lovely! We'll have dosa, jackfruit, and sambar for breakfast!"

I raced out the courtyard door once more, stopping at the base of the jackfruit tree and grasped one of the lower branches. I hoisted myself up onto it, gripping the trunk for balance.

A certain jackfruit caught my eye. It was plump, ripe, and almost half the size of Mishi, who was playfully swinging on the same branch. I was thankful that it was in my reach because I would not have been able to climb to the higher branch to pick it.

I slowly eased onto my tiptoes, knowing that the last thing Amachy wanted me to do was break a bone.

"When you pick a jackfruit, you always want to twist, not tear it off," was what she told me when she taught me to pick a jackfruit.

I played her words over and over again in my head as I twisted it off the massive fruit off the tree. That action reminded me, strangely enough, of the man who drove the school bus and how he would twist the steering wheel the same way that I twisted jackfruits. Things were so similar, yet so different.

I hadn't realized that I had already twisted the fruit off of the tree because I had been wound up in thought. I felt as though I were a bird flying down to her nest with blueberries for her young ones as I hopped down onto solid ground with the jackfruit.

"Amachy!" I cried, bursting into the house. "Look at the jackfruit I picked!"

Amachy looked up from the dosa pan, her eyes widening in astonishment. "My word! That's larger than Rudhi Gheet's prize winning one! How on Earth did you get it down?"

"I just hopped down," I shrugged, feeling very proud of myself. I wanted to boast, but I couldn't bring myself to do it. I remember when my twin brother, Nikhil, discovered a thicket of grapes in the courtyard. He boasted beyond belief! I envied him-- all anyone talked about was his grapes! But after nearly two days, his grapes started to taste acerbic— from sweet to sour grapes so quickly.

"Here, give it to me. I'll hack it open," Amachy offered, taking the jackfruit from me. "Oops! Can you flip that dosa? It would be a shame to waste it."

I scampered to the stove, grabbing a plastic spatula along the way.

"Loosen up the edges before you flip it," she reminded me.
I worked the spatula around the edges of the pan, slipping it under the dosa. Finally, I quickly flipped it onto another plate that was piled high with dosas.

"Perfect! I think we have plenty of dosas!" I declared, turning off the heat.

Amachy glanced at the plate. "I think we do. I'm glad that they're nice and thin. The last batch that I made was far too thick."

"Not true. The last batch you made was plenty thin. You can't get them anywhere else!"

"Oh, I'm sure that you find better ones, in, let's say England."

"England? How did we get to the topic of England? None of us have even been to England, let alone eaten a dosa there."

"Not yet…" she said, avoiding my eye contact and twiddling her fingers.

"Sorry?" I said, a quizzical mask plastered to my face.

"Nina, sometimes you have to be open to things changing. It helps us all achieve goals and learn more about our world."

She then abruptly turned away and said in a strained voice, "Go wake up Nikhil and your parents. Nothing is worse than breakfast gone cold."

I nodded in response and hurried to Nikhil's room, pondering what Amachy had said. I told myself to forget about it, as she was probably joking, for all of us knew that we could never leave India. The idea was absurd. It was our home, where we belonged. No other place would satisfy us as much as India.

"Nikki! Breakfast is ready! Tell Mummy and Daddy."

"Sure," Nikhil yawned, rubbing his eyes. "You woke me up."

"Sorry!" I apologized just before I speedily hurried back into the kitchen, where Amachy had been scooping the jackfruit seeds into a large bowl.

"Would you bring over the dosas, Nina?" she called.

"Love to," I replied.

I walked to the small stove and picked up the plate of dosas. My mouth was watering. It would be so easy just to snag one for myself before anyone else and say that Nikhil did it, but I would be lying, and lying brings you sour grapes just as boasting does.

I placed the plate of dosas down on the kitchen table right as Mummy, Dad, and Nikhil came in one by one.

"Good morning," Amachy welcomed them, just as she had for me. "We've got dosas, sambar, and a huge jackfruit that Nina picked."

I was glad that Amachy gave me credit. It showed the others that even though I was small, I could pick a jackfruit. Maybe Mummy would even let me pick the coconuts later today!

"Jackfruit's my favorite!" Dad exclaimed as he sat down at the small table, the corners of his mouth turning up.

"Well, what are you waiting for? Eat, eat, before it gets cold!" Amachy cried, gesturing for us to start.

I forked a dosa onto my stainless steel plate and a scoop of sambar as well. I would have the jackfruit as a sort of dessert later on. I tore off a piece of dosa and dipped it into the sambar. I could already smell all my favorite spices in the sambar. I popped the piece into my mouth, flavors exploding: turmeric, cumin, coriander. It felt like every spice in the spice drawer was in there, working together in some crazy way. I could hear murmurs of approval from around the table including mine. Amachy always made every meal better than the last!

After everyone had returned for second and third helpings of dosa and had just began to start on the jackfruit, my father stood up and cleared his throat, "As you know, I have been working at Vikram Motors for some time now. The company has been very satisfied with my work, and...and...I'm getting promoted to head sales manager!"

My gasp filled the air, but it was drowned out by the cheers and congratulation from everyone else. Head sales manager was a huge honor! It was like being the CEO, only of sales!

"But," he began. "My boss told me that if I wanted the position, then I would have to move to the United Kingdom location."

There was silence for a few minutes as we all processed that. Amachy had hinted that earlier! Were they both playing a joke? Or did he really mean that we would leave India?

"We leave tomorrow," my father meekly said. "I didn't tell you kids earlier because I knew this would be very hard. I thought telling you at the last minute would be easier. I hope you'll understand. We can call all your friends to say goodbye today and keep in touch. We are in seats 23A, 23B, 23C and 24A on Air India."

I could only process his last words.

"But that's only four seats," I blurted out. "There are five of us!"

My parents glanced at each other, and then Amachy.

"No!" I cried, tears welling in my eyes. "Amachy will be alone!"

"Sweetie," Amachy consoled me. "Your parents and I have known that this would happen weeks ago when your father told us. I have the house, and I'm the only pharmacist in town. Besides, what would I do in a place like England? You can save up your allowance to come visit me and Mishi in the summers!"

I rushed over to her and wrapped in a big bear hug, following Nikki's lead.

"Promise you won't forget us?" Nikki asked through a choked throat.

"Upon your grandfather's grave," she promised.

"Kids? You have to go pack. Amachy will help you," my mother whispered. "The suitcase that you'll share is in Nina's room."

Amachy walked out of the room with my father and Nikki, leaving my mother and me alone.

I turned toward her and said." I don't understand why we are doing this. Is it really worth the extra money to leave Amachy behind? How could you leave her here?"

My mother was speechless for a few seconds and then said in a firm voice, "Nina, life is hard. Sometimes, we make choices that will be better for us in five or ten years, not necessarily now. This is a small town and the future here is limited for you and Nikhil. Amachy wants the best for you. We would have never thought about leaving India and her if she did not want us to go."

Now, it was my turn to be speechless.

"Come!" Amachy yelled in a cheery voice from the bedroom.

I knew that she was trying to make us feel better; who knew when we would see her again? I walked slowly to the bedroom.

"Nikhil! Bring your clothes to Nina's room. Your parents will be packing everything else later."

"Okay," Nikhil yelled back.

No one wanted to leave India, but even more, no one wanted to leave Amachy. Yet, we knew that we must follow her directions, big and small.

"Nina, put your clothes on the right half so Nikki can have the left," she instructed as Nikhil walked in. "No one gets more, no one gets less."

Nikhil and I both did as we were told. We deliberately went as slow as possible in order to stretch our remaining time with Amachy.

"Mummy! Mummy!" someone called from the kitchen.

"That's your mother," Amachy said. "I'll go see what she wants."

Nikhil and I watched as Amachy strode out the door, and then turned to each other.

"Do you think that England will be all kings and queens and palaces like we learned in school?"

"More or less," I guessed. "We've hardly been out of the town, let alone another country."

"Do you truly believe that we'll ever see Amachy again?"

"I do, but we might be teenagers when we do."

"Do you think she really wants us to leave?"

That question left me speechless for a few minutes. I knew that Amachy wanted the best for our family and thought we should leave because of what my mother had told me, but would Amachy think we were abandoning her in a way? After all, she had taken care of Nikhil and me for the almost all our lives of our life when our parents were busy working long hours.

"I don't know, Nikki," I lied.

I spent the rest of the afternoon and evening packing clothes, toys, books. My parents thought I would want to say good bye to my friends, but I could not bear to see them. I went to bed that night drained, knowing that it was the last night in my bedroom, and I would have to savor it.

When I woke up the next morning, I was afraid to get out of bed, but I knew I had to rise.

Finally, I dressed and followed the noise to the hallway.

"Kids! The van is here!" my father shouted.

"We're leaving so soon?" I mouthed to Nikhil, who mouthed back, "It appears so!"

"Kids, say goodbye to Amachy," my mother quietly said. Nikhil hugged Amachy tight, not letting go until she had to ease him off.

I bound her in a hug too, staining her soft sari with my tears. Why couldn't she come with us? Of course I knew the answer, but still…

"Nina? We have to go," Nikhil whispered to me.

"Okay," I sighed, unwillingly pulling away from Amachy. "Promise you'll call and write every week?" I asked.

"I'll refuse when pigs fly," she answered, smiling at all of us. "Don't be late for the van."

My mother and father prodded us out after they said their goodbyes, taking twice as much time as we did. We couldn't blame them though; we would have done the same if we could.

After the driver had honked three times, we reluctantly towed our suitcases to the van. I felt like crying, but that would only make things worse. *Build a dam for your tears*, I told myself. *And don't let it break.*

198

"Goodbye, Mummy!" my mother yelled from the car.

"Thank you for everything, Padma!" my father, I think, thanked her.

"Say goodbye to Mishi for me!" Nikhil yelled. I wanted to do the same, but I was choked with tears.

The cab pulled away, leaving me with one last glimpse of Amachy smiling a rueful smile with tears down her face. I vowed to remember that smile, for it was the last one of hers I would see in a very, very long time.

I stared at the streets of India, thinking of how beautiful they looked, despite the litter. Oh, how I would miss everyone and everything in my small town. I never would forget it, no matter how much England might change me. I would always be from Thiruvella, India.

Screech! The van made a sudden stop in front of a red light. I heard the driver muttering something about a cyclist who cut him off before the light.

I gazed out the window once again, knowing that I had some time to kill before the next green light. I recognized Amachy's pharmacy shop with its pine green shutters and worn down sign that read: Thiruvella Pharmacy. How many memories I had made there! I would always come there after school to do my homework and help with customers. I always looked forward to it, staying there late into the evenings with Amachy and Nikhil. We didn't think of it as work; we thought of it as fun.

The van jolted forward, leaving me surprised as the shop disappeared out of sight. *Don't let the dam break*, I warned myself, but it was too late. Silent tears were already streaming down my face and onto the shabby seats. My mother noticed and enveloped me in a hug, her warmth radiating to me. I knew that it was supposed to make me feel better, but it only made me feel even more nostalgic and gloomy. Amachy hugged me in the same way.

"We're here!" my father called, waving his hands to get us moving and into the airport.

He undid the nylon cord that kept the trunk closed and handed Nikhil our suitcase, keeping his and my mothers for him to carry.

"We can switch off who takes it," Nikhil offered, handing me the suitcase. "I'll take it once we get through Customs."

We made it through Customs relatively quickly. I handed Nikhil the suitcase, and we both agreed that I would take it after Security.

It was my first time ever in an airport, and Nikhil's as well. We had only heard of the rest of the world, never had we seen it. News of all the amazing places around the world wafted into our small town through the internet and newspapers. Still, I never really wanted to live anywhere else. I loved my little town in India even if it didn't have kings, queens, castles or skyscrapers.

We whipped through Security just as quickly as we had through Customs. Nikhil gave the suitcase back to me, which I would take until we got to the terminal.

"Come on, our flight boards at 11:22 and it's 11:18 now!" my dad exclaimed, hustling us along. "There's no time to waste!"

We made it to the terminal at exactly 11:22, feeling quite fortunate due to the fact that we scored the second spot in line. No way were we expecting that!

"Next!" the lady at the desk called, motioning for us to come forward.

"Boarding pass and passport," she demanded.

"Right here," my dad replied, fishing them out of his backpack.

The lady peeked at each passport and scanned each boarding pass in record time, her hands never still. She handed us the passports and passes, then gestured for us to carry on into the tunnel that supposedly led to the plane.

200

"Give me the suitcase," commanded Nikhil. I handed it over, feeling quite claustrophobic, as there were no windows.

"Nikki, be careful," my mother warned him as he lugged the suitcase over a small gap in between the end of the tunnel and the entrance of the plane.

"Anjali, do you want to take the kids and I'll sit on my own?" my father asked my mother as we quickly walked through the narrow aisle.

"Sure," she agreed. "We're all next to each other anyway."

I admired the other planes from my window seat, noticing that one had a picture of a jackfruit on it. It reminded me of the jackfruit I had picked yesterday, the one that Amachy sliced. Oh, Amachy, how I missed her already! I felt tears welling up in my eyes, pushing to get out. *Don't cry*, I warned myself. *Build an even stronger dam for your tears.*

The plane jolted backwards, giving me a scare, and before I knew it we were in the air. "Look at the view!" Nikhil exclaimed, bouncing up and down in his seat.

"It's really quite magnificent," my mother agreed.

It really was a magnificent view, but I wasn't thinking about that. I was thinking about whom I had refused to say goodbye to India: my two best friends Geetha and Chetna, my teacher, Mishi, the bread vendor, and countless others. I had refused to say goodbye to the morning dew, the crow of the chickens, the corners of Amachy's eyes that crinkled when she laughed.

I had refused to say goodbye to India.

It's not too late to do it now, I said to myself. *Do it while you can.*

Goodbye, India.

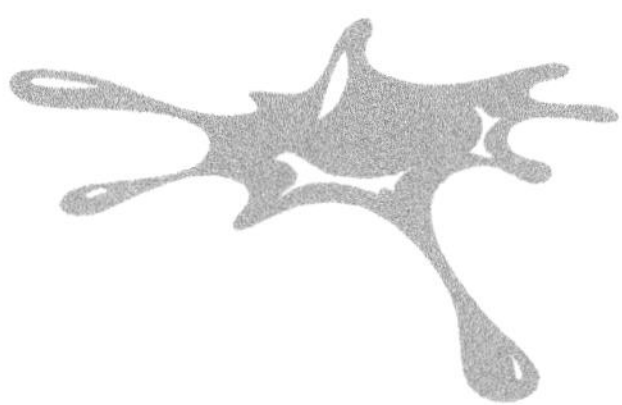

202

Plot Clarification

Patrick York mentored Benjamin Bouie through a revision focused on organizing events around the climax of his story, "The Shadow of the Dragon."

Dear Reader,

I had a great time revising "The Shadow of the Dragon" with Benjamin.

In this revision, we focused on plot clarification leading up to a climax. This might sound complex, so let me explain. Benjamin has a great way of creating exciting scenes, like the opening of the story when Momo flies across the treetops, then swoops down and eats a shark whole. What a wild event!

There's never a dull moment in "The Shadow of the Dragon." Because there were so many strong individual parts of his story, we focused on how those scenes were organized. In any story, you have a beginning, middle, and end. Somewhere between the middle and the end is a climax, which is the most exciting part of the story. In order for that moment to feel as if it is the most exciting, it is important for each of the scenes leading up to the climax to escalate—another word for "build."

Think of the game Jenga, for example. You start with all of the blocks in the tower, then you and your friend take turns removing one piece at a time. As each piece is removed from the tower, the game becomes more and more exciting. When will it fall over? Oh no! It's shaking! Be careful! Then, bam! It all goes over. The moment it falls is the climax: the most exciting part.

I had a great time working on this story, and I think Benjamin has a great way of engaging the imagination of the reader while delivering a heartwarming conclusion. This revision helped sharpen the scenes of the story and clarify the climax, allowing

the audience to experience the happiness of reuniting with family that you have intended here.

Happy Reading,
Patrick

Patrick York is from the Mojave Desert of California. He received his MFA from the University of California, Riverside where he was a Gluck Fellow of the Arts. He lives in Los Gatos, California with his wife.

Do you ever get to a point where you feel stuck?

Kind of. Sometimes I get to a point where I'm writing this piece that sounds really good. Then I think, *What do I write next? I could come up with something to write next, but will it be the best thing? Will it fit in?*

When that happened, what was your solution?

I either changed what I wrote before, which was really sad because it was a piece that I was really excited about, or I thought for five minutes.

Are you working on any other projects?

I am writing another story for school, but not free-writing. We're studying Shakespeare, which has a lot to do with writing. I'm writing this story, and my main character is William and he's a blacksmith. So the story is like the adventures of William the blacksmith.

When you write for the contest and when you write for school, what's the difference? Does it feel different?

I like free-writing better because it's not an assignment. I have fun writing anything, but when you get to write on your own, it all comes from your mind. It's not something that is assigned to you.

Do you ever think about plotting your stories, like we did, when you are writing for school?

I'm not really writing the story as much right now because we're focusing on poetry, but when I do write the story, I do focus on plot a little bit more.

208

As someone who has and a publishing experience like this as young as you are, what kind of advice would you give to other young writers?
I don't really know. I didn't really learn to write. When I started reading, I thought, *Maybe I should try this.* So I gave it a shot and it was easy, so I just dove in.

The Shadow of the Dragon

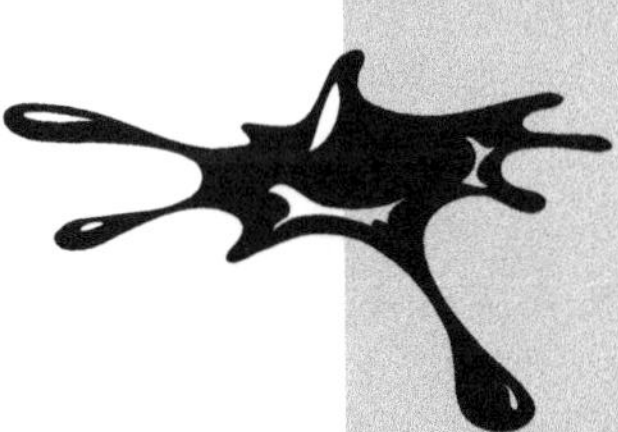

by

Benjamin Bouie

212

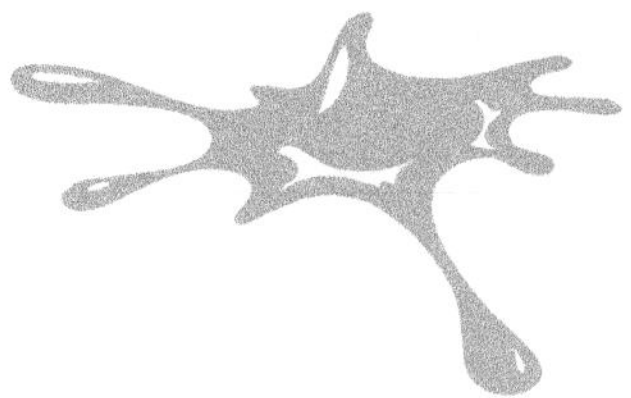

Part 1: When a Dragon Travels

Momo sat in his cave alone. He wished he was with his parents like he was five years ago. They would know whether he should go look for his friend Hunter and whether they could help each other. He had been thinking whether he really wanted to go look for his parents. He didn't think he would find them, but it was worth the try.

The next day, Momo woke up early. He started flying. He flew over the trees. He had to fly from the Redwood Circle, which is a part of Treeville, all the way to that little island in Canada! He heard all sorts of noises. Then, bang, boom, clang, clash!! A shark leapt out of the water.

Momo heard someone say, "Woo hoo!"

Momo saw a fishing boat. On the boat, were two men. The men had caught a shark, which was Momo's favorite food. Momo was pretty small for a dragon, but to the men, he looked like a giant flying lizard. When Momo saw the shark, he dove down and put out his super sharp talons. The men ducked. As any dragon would do, he grabbed the shark. At this point, he was very, very hungry. He hadn't had any breakfast and last night, he hadn't had any dinner. He swallowed the shark whole. He then caught a new shark and offered it to the men. One of them wrinkled his nose in disgust as the other one fainted. Momo ate the shark and flew away.

Momo saw a helicopter. A human jumped out and landed on a nearby island with a soft thump. Momo knew it was Hut. Hut's real name was Hunter.

"Let's go!" said Momo.

"But, but…," said Hut.

"Let's go!"

"Okay, okay," said Hut.

"We have to go and find that dragon! And I will give you a ride!" said Momo. "If you want my help to find your brother, don't be such a show-off like when you jumped out of the helicopter."

"I'm not," said Hut.

"Yeah, right, but let's just go to the World of Rocks," said Momo.

"No way, I'm not going anywhere!" said Hut.

"Do you want me to leave?" said Momo.

"No," said Hut, "But….but, I want to…"

Hut looked around for a reason not to go because he was scared and remembered that it was cold in the World of Rocks. Meanwhile, Momo was thinking about the journey ahead of them. They heard a noise, but couldn't see anything because the fog was so thick. Even Momo couldn't see through the mist with his sharp eyesight. He thought they should go.

"What do you want?" said Momo.

"I'm only 13, I need rest!" said Hut.

"Okay, we'll both take a rest," said Momo.

"Wait, you're planning on going halfway across the galaxy with a map?" asked Hut.

"No, I'm not, but that is one of my main supplies," said Momo.

"What do you mean 'supplies'?" said Hut.

"Okay, let's just go," Momo said.

Two minutes later, they were flying high above the clouds, Hut resting on Momo's back. When they landed in the World of Rocks, it was almost midnight. Now, you might wonder how a dragon can go, as Hut said, "halfway across the galaxy" in a few hours. Well, here's the answer: Lightning dragons can fly at supersonic speed and Momo was a lightning dragon.

"Stop it," said Momo.

"Stop what?" said Hut.

"Not you. Look!" said Momo.

"Huh?" said Hut.

"Hut, take out your bow!"

A giant serpent slithered past them so close that it nearly knocked Hut over and then they noticed a battle gnome was charging after it. It was about the size of Hut's head.

He was yelling "yawwww!"

The serpent ran headlong into a tree. But the one that came next was even bigger!

"Wow, this place sure does have a lot of serpents," said Hut.

Momo dashed after it as Hut talked to the gnome. Then Hut,

Momo and the gnome ran after the serpent. The serpent disappeared.

"Goodbye," said the gnome. He vanished into thin air.

Boom! A huge asteroid hit the trees. A hooded figure stared at them.

"Hey Momo," said Hut. "Do you think that asteroid has something to do with that?"

A bunch of robots were heading towards them. Hut fell to his knees. Hut's weakness was robots. A centaur that looked like a soldier from the World of Rocks leapt through the air and kicked its back legs at the robots. The robots ran away and the centaur solider, whoever he was, ran in the other direction.

"I am master of the serpents," said an evil, cold voice, "Lord Fangling."

"Lord What?" said Hut.

"Attack!" said Momo.

The hooded figure emerged from the shadows. Hut screamed. His face was twisted and his eyes were like a snake's. He laughed a long, cold, evil laugh. Lord Fangling was Momo's father's friend, but the master of serpents and Momo's father got into an argument about whether dragons or serpents were better, and Lord Fangling turned evil.

"I have waited a long time for this," said Lord Fangling.

"Hut, Hut?" said Momo.

Hut was a whimpering heap on the ground. Then Momo lost his temper.

"Hut, get up and stop messing around!"

"I want to go home," said Hut.

"Well, we'll go home when we stop this maniac!" said Momo.

"Okay," said Hut.

Momo shot a bolt of lightning at Lord Fangling. He shrank into the shadows. A golden spark went up.

"We have to follow those sparks!" said Momo. "My family is near and so is yours."

Hut knew he was right.

"Momo, you just told ME to calm down," said Hut.

"Hey, what's that stuff on the ground?" said Hut.

"Unicorn blood," said Momo.

There was no mistaking that silver liquid, well, at least for a dragon. Momo had been in the wild most of his life and Momo knew all the signs of nature. Momo and Hut followed the trail of unicorn blood, then they saw a small patch of trees. Hut peeled back the branches so Momo could see.

"What the…" said Hut.

In the clearing was a magnificent sight: Two fully grown dragons!

Part II: The Dragon Comeback

One of the dragons was leaning over a wounded unicorn. The other was giving it something to eat. One of the dragons stood up and spotted Momo.

He came over and spoke in a deep voice, "You can come, the human has to stay."

"But…" said Momo.

"That is enough!" said the dragon.

"But he is my friend!" said Momo.

"I said that is enough! He is a human, he must go," said the dragon.

"But he is not a normal human, he does not threaten dragons like the others." said Momo.

"Hmmmm, okay," said the dragon. "But, he needs a place to sleep," said the dragon.

"Thank you!" said Hut.

Later that day, the dragon said something that made Momo wonder aloud, "Who are you?" Momo didn't mean to say it, but the words escaped his brain.

"Me? Well," the dragon said, sitting down on a log, "I am a dragon warrior, but you can call me Thorgon. But, you're sure you don't know me? You look familiar."

"No, but what's up with that unicorn?" said Momo.

"We found an injured unicorn. Come on, time for bed," said Thorgon. He clearly wanted to change the subject.

That night, Momo couldn't sleep, so he decided to go for a walk to wait off his feelings. But, when he was starting to get tired, he got the feeling he was being watched, and out of the corner of his eye, his saw a pair of big, brown eyes! He spun around on his feet. The eyes were gone, and when he was hoping he was seeing things, he heard a rustling in the leaves.

"I am definitely not alone," he said to himself. "Or, am I just tired?"

He thought that the thing that was scurrying around in the leaves must have heard him because he could not hear the rustling anymore.

"Maybe I should go back to Hut, Thorgon and that other dragon."

And then, he walked off.

The next day, Momo woke up looking tired, but perfectly happy.

"You look troubled. Need my help?" said Thorgon.

"No, it's nothing," said Momo casually. "Just a little tired."

"A little?" said Thorgon, looking surprised at Momo's behavior. Momo was about to get to the point. Thorgon must have read Momo's mind because he said, "Well, Momo, I bet you didn't know, but I am your father."

Momo's jaw dropped. "What?!" said Momo.

"And the other dragon is your mother," said Thorgon.

Then, there was a rustling in the leaves.

"This place is creepy," said Momo.

A man appeared from the shadows. Surprisingly, somehow, it looked like Hut, except instead of a bow and arrow, he had a sword. And, he had big round circles around his eyes, which looked like glasses.

"TTTTooooom?" said Hut.

"Hut?" said the man.

They ran up to each other and hugged each other as if they were brothers. At this point, Momo thought they were.

The man said, "I'm Tom, but call me Shadow Man."

Momo had a feeling that this was what had rustled in the bushes the night before. And, he thought that this time he would live with his family and Hut's family forever.

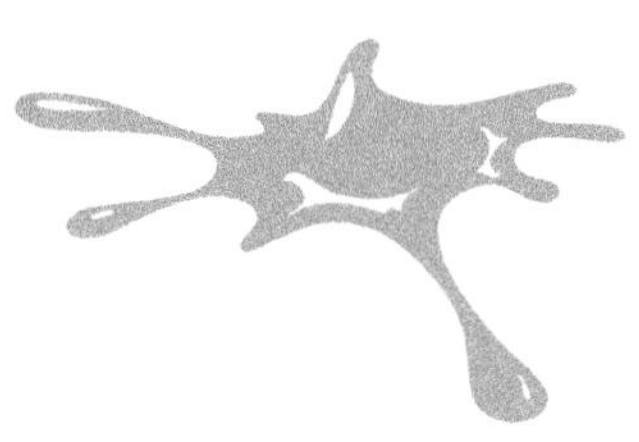

220

Scene Versus Summary

Helen Pyne worked with Sonia Kulasooriya Camacho on transforming the events of her story, "Friend," into scenes that show the reader what her characters are experiencing.

Dear Reader,

When I first read Sonia's poignant story, "Friend," I was drawn in by the narrator's distinctive voice. Sonia did an excellent job of capturing her protagonist's interior thoughts and emotions and using descriptive language and images to enhance her setting and scenes.

The trouble was, there weren't enough scenes in the story; there was way too much summary instead. The main character, Beatriz, was telling us what happened through her memories. This distanced the reader and kept us from fully engaging with the character, since we weren't experiencing her struggles firsthand. So I chose scene vs. summary for our revision focus and asked Sonia to show us how Beatriz felt by changing some of her thoughts into scenes.

Typically, a scene shows and a summary tells. Both are methods of treating time in fiction, but each has its place and purpose. Summary can give readers information about a character, her background, motive, or history. It can also help a writer skip over periods of time that aren't important to the story, ranging from an hour to many years. In contrast, a scene happens in real time and can include dialogue, actions, physical movements, smells, sounds, etc. When Sonia's frightened protagonist, Beatriz, walks into her new school, and "a billion necks turn and a billion pairs of eyes stare," this is a terrific moment in scene. The reader is there, experiencing what she experiences.

Writing new scenes solved several problems. First, the dialogue added tension and humor. Second, Beatriz's interactions with the other characters added interest

and insight. (Initially, Beatriz's mother was a remote, shadowy figure, who said nothing. After the revision, we were able to see the loving mother-daughter relationship through dialogue and body language.) Third, Sonia's fabulous physical descriptions helped to ground the story and make the setting feel real.

Sonia also used setting to reflect her narrator's emotional state. When Beatriz felt scared, for example, the school looked ugly and intimidating. When Beatriz felt happy, the school became a beautiful place. This way, instead of naming emotions—like happy, sad, scared, or mad—writers can show us by describing objects or places—a concept also known as the "objective correlative." In addition, we fixed time discrepancies, cut and pruned to tighten the writing, and changed all verbs to the present tense.

"Friend" is a story is about a young girl's transformation. Changing passive summaries into active scenes can transform your writing too!

Happy Writing,
Helen Pyne

Helen Pyne has always loved making up stories. Growing up, she staged plays, performed magic shows and designed haunted houses in the basement of her house. She's rappelled down cliffs in Alaska, traveled in a hot air balloon in Africa and eaten scorpions-on-a-stick in China, but she thinks reading is the biggest adventure of all. Helen has a B.A. in English from Middlebury College and an M.F.A. in creative writing for children and young adults from Vermont College of Fine Arts. The mother of four children, she is the author of two young adult mystery novels and works as a writer and editor.

Sonia Kulasooriya Camacho

Sonia is a twelve year old 6th grader who goes to Corte Madera School. She comes from a multicultural family. Her mom is from Spain and her dad is from Sri Lanka. Sonia enjoys reading, writing, drawing, and spending quality time with her family and friends. Sonia's favorite animals are deer, because they symbolize peace, kindness, and gentleness to her. She lives in Woodside, California.

Here are some of Sonia's thoughts on the writing and revision of "Friend."

How did you come up with the idea for "Friend"?

I came up with the idea for "Friend" at school. Many of my friends get bullied for being themselves, and I've always wanted to stop it. For "Friend," all I did was take one of my memories and add the background of being a bully victim. I wanted to show people how much bully victims suffer, so that it will help others understand and try to help.

What changed in your story when you turned sections of summary into scene?

When I converted paragraphs of summary into scene, I think it put in a lot more emotion. Basically, it helped the

reader to understand more of all the emotions Beatríz was feeling.

What was the hardest part of the revision for you?

For me, the hardest part of the revision was knowing when summary had to be changed into scene, how long it should be, and why it had to be there in the first place. Most of my stories are written completely in scene, so I had no idea, at first, how to change any of the paragraphs.

What did you learn from this process that you can use when you write your next story?

I learned that you have to look at the story as a reader. The reader isn't going to know the whole plot. Now I look at all of the different angles of the story, not just at the writer's point of view. And if that's too hard, I'll let one of my friends or family members look at it and tell me what they think.

How long have you been writing fiction and what do you like best about writing?

I started really getting into writing fiction around six years old. My first story was about two girls on Halloween who go trick-or-treating and meet a friendly ghost. They have to help the ghost find a special possession and return back home in time for dinner. I've always loved writing fiction and fantasy because you can do anything you want. There are no limits to writing. In my opinion, writing has always been fun to me because it's like creating your own world.

Do you have any advice for other young writers?

Never give up on a story! If you find yourself stuck at a writing block, let your mind flow loose for a while. It may take a few hours, or even days, for you to get another idea, but don't stop writing. I always find it easiest to prevent writing blocks by writing out a short summary of the whole story. Use one of those writing charts they give you at school and think of the beginning, middle, and end. However, if you're writing a very long story with lots of chapters, you may want to make a more complex story chart that explains each chapter.

Friend

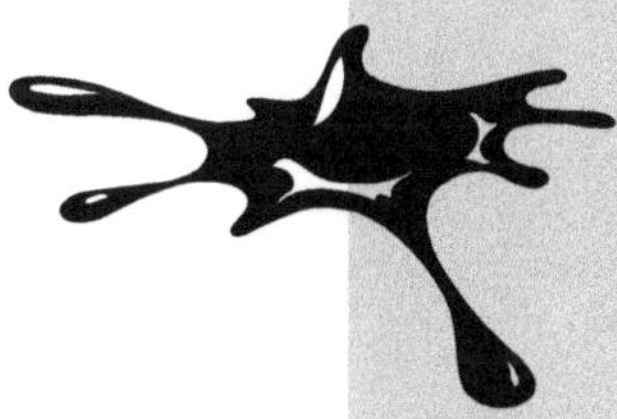

by

Sonia Kulasooriya Camacho

230

Prologue

Words. Question. Thoughts. He teases me. He says I am not the same. He tells me that I am nothing. Why? I did not say anything to him. He only said things to me. Why can't I speak up? Why can't I tell him to stop? I want to, but I can't. I just can't. Why?

Words swirl around me, out of my reach, unable to escape my lips. Beautiful words, like a rose. Delicate, like a snowflake. Powerful, like a lion. Thoughtful words. Smart words. Kind words.

Determined. Brave. Cheerful. Quiet. Interesting. Tender. Shy. Calm.

I keep hiding, running away from what tries to pull me into the darkness. The shadows wrap around me, but I will not let them. No more running. No more hiding. It's time for a change in my world. A big change.

Meaningful. Strong. Different. New.

It's a typical gray, gloomy morning in Portola Valley. The sky is exactly the shade of the gray and silver woolen scarf Mami has wrapped snugly around her neck. The weak, white sun peeks out of a bundle of clouds and smiles shyly at me. I wave to it timidly and tuck a dark curl behind my ear.

Why couldn't we just keep our old house and stay there? Why do I even have to go to another school? And why of all things was this ugly brown jacket the first thing I grabbed?

Mami's glossy black high heels click eerily against the dull cement ground, turning the silence of the intimidating, large building in front of me even more intense and frightening. She sighs and bends down, brushing the hair out of my face gently.

"Beatríz. Beatríz, *cariño*, darling, look at me." I stop walking to look at Mami's face. She is very pretty, my Mami. Mami has dark hair that falls onto her face like thick, shining waterfalls. Her skin is olive and glows with healthiness. Mami's beautiful castaño eyes shine with love. They are so beautiful, her eyes. Light brown with specks of bright, pure gold.

"Listen, mi vida. Think of this school as a new beginning, algo nuevo. Darling, please do not worry. It will go faster than you can imagine, y en unos días solo, vas a tener amigas nuevas. Just a few days, cariño, you won't be alone anymore. This is a good school, I promise. Te lo prometo."

I sniff, gazing into Mami's warm eyes. She smiles and pulls me into a warm hug. It feels good. It feels like I could just melt into her arms, and never face the harsh world full of its cruel lies. It feels like I could just stay in third grade forever and never grow up. But it's not like that… no. Now I am in fourth grade. Now I have to grow up.

We are almost there. The parking lot is so large, I think it will never end. I blink furiously and battle with the tears that threaten to spill out. White coils of mist roll lazily around the school, tingling coolly against my creamy coffee-colored skin, as if I have just jumped into a frozen lake and then quickly been rubbed dry with a towel.

Suddenly, the clicking stops. The large building looms high above me, the building Mami is telling me I must now enter. I feel like I'm underwater. I can't hear Mami properly. Taking a step would require a miracle. Voices tug at my mind, frantic thoughts cloud the common sense section of my brain. I can't move. I clench my hands into fists, my fingernails digging into my palms. My legs are numb with dread, my voice is blocked with emotion, my breaths become quicker and quicker, making me dizzy. I can't do this…I can't…can't do this…no… Flashes of their smirking faces, their taunting voices, their hurtful words…

The boy. His name was… Thomas. Thomas had copper brown hair, and dark, cold, cruel eyes…Those eyes alone would whip at your face with freezing blasts of hate. The pleasure in those horrible eyes…the pleasure…it only showed after he had torn a delicate flower from its stem, a child from its happiness, a feather from a graceful bird.

I remember…I remember…

They're gone! GONE! They will not hurt me anymore! They are gone…

Mami is hugging me now. Her warm arms embrace me with so much love that it almost washes away all the pain…Almost. She is saying goodbye now. It is more than a goodbye…Mami, Mami who loved me for as long as I can remember, is letting me go. She is the mother bird. I am the baby bird. And she is letting me fly away…

I burn with determination. I can do this…I can! I swim strongly against the thick currents of fear and anxiety that threaten to engulf me with each kick. The shadows try to bring me back into the darkness, but I am DONE with the darkness and the shadows. It is time to go into the light.

I reach the surface and take a deep breath. It's going to be alright. Finally I have reached the shore. The shore of Indian Creek Elementary.

I pull the cold, silver handle of the gymnasium door and step inside quietly as I possibly can. The door shuts silently behind me, but I feel like a bomb just exploded. A billion necks turn, a billion pairs of eyes stare, and I turn to stone. I turn slowly and face the large, glass doors, only to see Mami walking away…away from me….

I turn again to look at the people staring at me. Without knowing what to do, I simply shiver inside my large jacket. So I just stand there, a little girl in her huge jacket shivering against a school full of staring children and teachers. The eyes are brown, blue, green, amber, hazel… large, wide, small, bright, intent…

All are different in some way. But all of the eyes are trained on me. The thought of curling up into a tight ball of humiliation tempts me. I want to so badly, but I don't. Finally, I hold my head up high and slowly drag my stubborn feet towards the nearest teacher. Her warm smile goes well with her long, amber hair and almond-shaped eyes.

"Hi, you must be Beatríz, right? The new fourth grade girl?"

I nod slowly and bite my lip nervously. The teacher pronounces Beatríz like Bee-yah-tris. Mami says my name like Bih-ah-triz, the right way. And the teacher has an American accent.

"Well we're just in the middle of an assembly, as you can see. Just sit down and the principal will finish up so we can go to class," she says cheerily.

"Where...where do I sit?" I whisper shakily. I try not to look afraid, though inside it feels like I'm fighting a war just to keep standing.

The teacher points over to an empty spot next to a cluster of girls. I shuffle to my spot and plop down, pulling the hood of my jacket down to hide my face. One of the girls stares at me and whispers into her friend's ear. I don't care. I just let the tears form a pool of sadness on my large jacket. I just want to be done with this.

I sit, for the first time, during an assembly at a school named after a creek. But I sit, not for the first time, without a single friend in the world except the sun and a teacher.

I soon realize that although the mornings were cold, it is steaming hot in Portola Valley during lunch. The chatter of fourth and fifth graders fills the air with happiness. I feel like there is a transparent force separating me from everyone else. Fortunately, those thoughts are pushed aside, thanks to a girl with bright orange hair and freckles. She breathlessly tells me to stay away from a girl named Alex Smithe with long brown hair, freckles, and brown eyes. I stare at her as she sprints away. Of course, I go looking for the girl named Alex Smithe, who wouldn't?

Soon enough I bump into a student. She stumbles and I blush shyly.

"Oh! Hi...sorry... I'm Beatríz. Do you know... um, where this girl is?" I whisper, groaning inside. *I forgot to describe the girl named Alex*

Smithe! I think frantically. The girl, who has long brown hair, brown eyes, and freckles, is beginning to look annoyed. But I push that aside. I hope she doesn't get mean. *Just in case she does, I'll try to sound more popular.*

"Um, sorry. She has long brown hair. Kinda like you," I state nonchalantly, trembling with humiliation inside. The girl studies me carefully.

"Okay, Beatríz... Tell me a bit more. There's a lot of girls in fourth grade with long brown hair," she replies coolly.

"Well, she has brown eyes, like you. And freckles, also like you," I add quickly.

The girl's face changes rapidly from annoyance to curiosity.

"Oh, and her name is Alex Smithe. Do you know where she is?"

A spark of amusement lights up the girl's face.

"Oh, I definitely know where Alex is." She laughs quietly.

Suddenly, the puzzle pieces begin to click inside my mind. I blink back tears of shame. It was just a question! One little question, and I blew it. This is Alex! Now she'll make fun of me for sure. I wait in silence for the teasing to follow. But she doesn't make fun of me. She is laughing with me instead.

Now, I like her a lot. She is pretty, with her long brown curls that she says are tipped with amber in the summer. Her eyes are hazelnut brown with a thin, misty layer of blue-gray that shades them brilliantly. One of her eyes are a darker shade of brown layered with blue-green. She has pale skin sprinkled with a healthy helping of freckles.

Alex tells me she has a boy's name and to not make fun of it. I assure her that I wouldn't dream of it. Despite our awkward meeting, she chooses to sit with me at my lonely table at lunch, when she could have easily picked the crowded table full of the other girls. But, yes, she sits with me. And, sure, she steals my fork and runs around with it. But she gives it back when I ask, which I didn't expect. She is different, but so am I. She is funny. She is kind. She is matter of fact. She is smart. She is my friend.

Suddenly, I feel the transparent force lift. Suddenly, the sky is transforming into a deep blue, the clouds turning into cotton, the sun beaming and showering me with warmth, the plants standing a little taller, the trees becoming brighter and more colorful, the students smiling at me, the flowers showing their blossoms. All at once, I could see the world as everyone else had.

And now I know...I know that nobody should ever be told that they cannot be who they are. Now I know that it is wrong to be mistreated if you are different. And if I ever get treated again the way I was before, it will stop!

For the first time, I let my past fly away in wisps like the gray clouds had just done. For the first time, I let myself enjoy true happiness. And for the first time, I have a real *friend*.

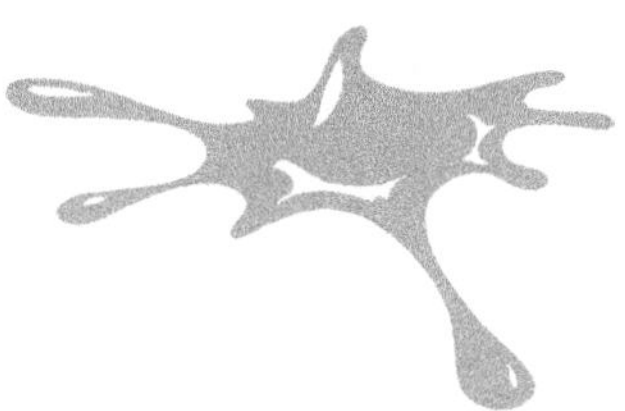

238

Using Actions to Show Character Feelings

Naomi Kinsman mentored Rachel Hoge through a revision focused on communicating characters' emotions through action in the story.

Dear Reader,

Rachel Hoge's "The Sheriff and the Tree House" is a full-of-fun fantastical adventure with twists and turns throughout. One of my favorite parts of this story is the main character, the very responsible sheriff. Although he fully enjoys his adventure, he also cares deeply about his family and his job, and he doesn't want to let anyone down—even when he finds himself unexpectedly in an alternate world.

Like many fantasies, Rachel's story started out with a lot of surprises and a fast-paced plot. We decided we wanted to keep the fast pace and all of the surprising magical happenings, while also making even more out of each scene. To do that, we pretended the sheriff was an actor and we were the directors of his story.

First, we broke the short story down into scenes and figured out what Rachel wanted the purpose of each scene to be. Then, we came up with stage directions and also props for each scene. The action and the interaction with objects in the setting helped to highlight the purpose of the scene. We asked ourselves questions such as, "If the sheriff were on stage and we asked him to 'do his job well,' what do we imagine the actor physically doing?" Would he walk up and down the rows of cells and check each jail cell to make sure it's really locked? Would he use his flashlight and peer into each cell to make sure the inmates aren't up to any mischief?

Rachel went over and above in her revision, and found some fun surprises along the way, for instance the sheriff's playful word-choice such as, "Wowskers!" All of the added action, dialogue and description helped us to get to know the character better. We both recommend that you try it yourself on your

own writing. How? Break your story into scenes and then read one. Close your eyes and picture the scene happening on stage. What do the actors do? What might a director coach them to add to make the scene even more interesting? Add your ideas to the scene, and then move on to the next. You'll find that through this staging process, your characters spring to vibrant life.

Happy Writing,
Naomi

Naomi Kinsman, Author of the *From Sadie's Sketchbook Series* and *Spilled Ink*, the award winning Inklings Writers' Notebook, is passionate about sharing her love of writing and creativity with young writers. Naomi's background in improvisational and story theatre as well as her arts education work in Chicago, Portland and the Bay Area has convinced her that creative play is a doorway through which learners can find inspiration and transformative learning experiences. Naomi loves to play in many ways, but some of her favorites are tap-dancing, sketching, experimenting in the kitchen and chasing her Portuguese Water Dog, Turley. Naomi has a BA in Theatre Arts from Seattle Pacific University and has studied theatre with the Piven Theatre Workshop and ACT. She also has a Masters in Writing for Children and Young Adults from Hamline University.

Rachel Hoge

Rachel Anne Hoge is nine years old and is the third child, out of four children in her family. She likes to play soccer, do gymnastics and swim. She also loves to read, write, ride fast crazy roller coasters and climb trees, walls, mountains, volcanoes or anything else you can climb. Rachel goes to Los Paseos Elementary School in San Jose, CA. Her favorite subject in school is math. She also likes ELA because a lot of the time her class reads a book and then writes an imaginative paragraph about the story. When she grows up, she wants to go to Brigham Young University to become a writer, a gymnast, a paleontologist or a teacher.

Here are some of Rachel's thoughts on the writing and revision of "The Sheriff and the Tree House."

Where do you like to write?

I like writing in my living room because there's lots of people in there doing lots of things and they give me lots of ideas of what to write about.

What kinds of books do you like to read?

I like a lot of the books by Beverly Cleary, the *Junie B. Jones* series and the *Ivy and Bean* books. I also like books with magic in them.

Was it difficult to revise your story?

Yes, it was hard to think of new ideas and more details to add to the story.

Do you think the new ideas and details made the story better?

Yes. I added more of what I imagined about what the Sheriff did when he got to the magical world. Also, the tree house was more hidden than it was before.

What does adding physical action to the description do for a story or for a character?

When you add action, it tells the reader how your character is exactly moving, and you can see how he feels.

What advice would you give other writers who want to make their stories exciting?

I would say to ask other people for ideas. Then, pick one of the ideas and add a little more detail of your own to expand that idea.

What do you like best about writing?

I like how I can use my imagination. I also like other people being able to read something exciting that I made up.

The Sheriff and the Tree House

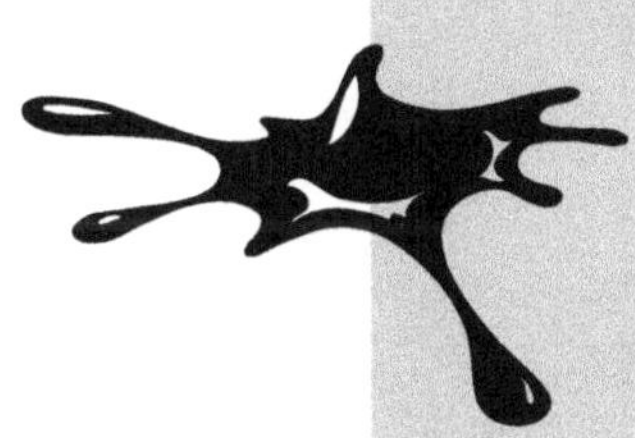

by

Rachel Hoge

246

Once there was a sheriff of a little town called Springville, Arizona. The sheriff did his job very well. Part of his job was to make sure his prisoners didn't escape. Every ten minutes, he patrolled up and down the halls, counting prisoners. One day his jail house was full. He went downstairs to look for some extra jail cells in the basement. It was dark, so he swung his flashlight around in circles on the walls to see what was down there.

He saw a door to the janitor's closet. He opened it, feeling very excited because he liked mysteries. He'd had his job for over three years and nobody had ever told him about the closet. When he opened the door, he saw cleaning supplies and also a hole in the wall which had light shining through it. He peeked through and saw a secret opening in the janitor's closet. It was a very dirty passageway. He was unsure if he should go through. The sheriff made a call to the assistant sheriff to watch the prisoners for him.

The Sheriff and the Tree House

The sheriff decided to go through the passage way. As he went through the opening, he walked carefully through the dirty passageway, watching his step. He almost stepped on a dead mouse that drowned in a puddle of spilt Clorox Bleach. There were mice, spiders and cockroaches everywhere. Apparently, the bleach wasn't doing its job. The janitor must have given up trying to clean the dirty passageway. The Sheriff was so disgusted that he wanted to go back.

Just as he was about to leave, he saw through the corner of his eye, a far bright light. The Sheriff was anxious to see what the bright light was. He was impatient and ran toward the bright light. As he got closer, he noticed the bright light was an opening to a beautiful place. He saw many wonderful things. One of the things he saw was a floating pathway of different colors. The colors on the pathway were red, yellow, blue and magenta. The sheriff noticed that the floating pathway had an upside down spiral staircase connected to it. He was suspicious and wondered how anyone could walk upside down and not fall off. The Sheriff was so curious that he had to try and climb it.

When he reached the staircase, he noticed strange neon tie-dye metal boots and a sign that read, *Wear Me.* He put on the boots and as he took his first step onto the staircase, he noticed the boots were walking for him. The boots were electronic and magnetic. The sheriff was a little scared walking upside down for the first time. He sure hoped he wouldn't fall. Luckily, he made it safely onto the colorful floating pathway. Suddenly, the boots disappeared off his feet. The Sheriff carefully followed the pathway for a while until it forked into two directions. If he went to the right, he noticed there was a beautiful indigo waterfall. If went to the left, it went through a dried-up forest. He decided to go right to the beautiful, majestic, indigo waterfall.

The Sheriff was amazed at the beauty of the waterfall. It was so pretty. He had never seen indigo-colored water before. He could hear the rushing sound of water and the sound of birds flying overhead. He couldn't believe his eyes when he noticed there were mermaids swimming and sliding down the waterfall.

The Sheriff pinched himself to see if he was dreaming, but he felt his pinch. He was not dreaming. This must be a magical land. The waterfall emptied into a lake below. The lake was a mermaid playground. Mermaids swam gracefully, slid down rocks and sun-bathed. As the Sheriff kept walking past the mermaid lake, it formed a river with a bridge over it. He walked over the bridge. It looked like it dead-ended into a wall of vines and bushes.

The Sheriff was curious to see what was past the vines. Why would a bridge dead-end into nothing? He pushed past the vines and bushes and noticed a shining, beautiful green tree with a rope ladder hanging down. The Sheriff definitely wanted to climb up the tree to see if that was magical too.

The sheriff climbed up into the tree house. It was very messy. In fact, it looked like the zoo had a party in the tree house. There were broken dishes, toys, soccer balls, baseballs, baseball bats, basketballs, roller skates left out and art supplies everywhere. The Sheriff had a hard time walking through the mess. There was so much stuff on the floor, it was like walking through a maze. He picked up a rotten banana peel and threw it out the window. As he was exploring the tree house, he saw buttons that were red, blue, yellow and green. With his eyes fixed on the buttons, he tripped on a wooden bat and fell on a button. All of a sudden, the tree house started to spin very fast. The sheriff slid into the corner of the tree house and held onto the corner walls. The tree house was spinning so fast that the sheriff began to feel sick. Finally the tree house stopped.

It took the sheriff a few minutes before he was able to stand up and look around. He blinked a few times and noticed he wasn't in Springville anymore. He carefully climbed down and figured he was probably in Hawaii. This place was the most magical place he had ever seen. He saw palm trees that looked like giant licorice sticks and gumdrops. The sheriff smelled the candy palm tree and took a lick. It tasted so good to him and thought the palm tree was made out of the world's best candy.

All of a sudden, something weird flew over his head. It was an animal that was half unicorn and half owl. The animal flew down next to the sheriff and asked him who he was. The Sheriff was shocked and afraid at first. He didn't know that animals could talk. The sheriff told the animal that he was a visitor from Springville, Arizona. The sheriff asked the half unicorn and half owl what kind of animal he was. The sheriff found out that it was a uniowl. He had never seen a uniowl before. The uniowl flew off fast. It wasn't very friendly.

The sheriff also saw a talking, walking mushroom, a flying blue and white talking Cheshire cat and something magically strange. It was changing from a pig into a horse. The Cheshire Cat said it was an oompaloompalu. This oompaloompalu could turn into anything it wanted to, such as a dog, a car, a bike, a plane, a hot air balloon, and a trampoline.

The sheriff said to himself, *I am never going to leave this place.*

250

Just as he said that to himself, the magical tree house started spinning and left him there.

At first, the sheriff panicked and ran everywhere he'd been. He looked around every corner, afraid he'd never find his way home. He was worried about his jail and his family that he left behind. They were probably worried about him, too. If he were to see the town of Springville right now, he would probably see missing sheriff signs posted everywhere.

He sat down against the tree and scratched the back of his neck. After a while, he decided not to worry so much and enjoy the magical land he was in. The sheriff ate all the fruit and candy he wanted because he could pick it off the trees. He slept in the tree hammocks and he played with the oompaloompalu. The oompaloompalu was the best friend a person could have. His favorite things to do with the oompaloompalu were to take turns pushing each other in the hammocks and to play tag and hide and go seek. They also liked making up funny phrases such as "Squashed Tomatoes!" "Pickles and Pie!" and "Pirates and Jellybeans!" The sheriff was having a great time, but six months later, he got tired of being in the magical world. He missed the town of Springville, Arizona and his family.

The sheriff said, "I wish the tree house was here to take me home."

To the sheriff's surprise, about five minutes after he said this, the tree house appeared.

"Wowskers!" shouted the shocked sheriff.

He climbed in and went to the control panel, but he wasn't sure which button to press to go home. He pressed the blue button and a rope swing came out.

"Argh!" he growled.

Next, he pushed the yellow button and fireworks came shooting out of the top of the tree house.

"Argh, argh!" he growled again, this time louder.

He pressed the green button and a water slide that led to a pool appeared. He kicked the wall and then hopped around, holding his toes because they hurt. Finally, he pushed the red button and the tree house started to spin. When it stopped, he was back in Springville, Arizona. The sheriff was finally back. After he rubbed his head and could finally see straight, he walked back towards the jail. It looked like the assistant sheriff didn't do a very good job, because he was sleeping and the jail cells were empty!

The sheriff woke up the assistant sheriff and asked, "Where did all the prisoners go?"

"Uhh… I don't know," the Assistant Sheriff said, shrugging.

"Where did all of the prisoners go?" demanded the Sheriff.

The assistant sheriff knew he was in big trouble. He looked around and saw a paperclip unfolded on the ground. He realized the prisoners must have picked the locks. All the cells were open and the prisoners had escaped. The sheriff fired the assistant sheriff on the spot and started looking for a new one.

The head sheriff was glad to be back in his hometown of Springville, Arizona. He was proud of his job, but he thought it would be fun to go on another trip next year to a new place filled with many adventures. Every once in a while, he checked the door in the janitor's closet to make sure it was there, ready and waiting.

The Heart of the Poem

Mandy Davis mentored Cynthia Wang through a revision focused on evoking emotion in the reader by focusing on the heart of her poem, "Cherry Blossoms at Tidal Basin."

Dear Reader,

Just like your heart is at the center of you, there should always be a big idea at the center of any piece of writing. This big idea, sometimes called the main idea or theme, is what the poem is all about. But the heart of the poem is more than just this big idea, it's also how this idea makes you feel.

Have you ever been reading a story or poem and

felt something? That's what happened to me when I was reading Cynthia Wang's poem "Cherry Blossoms at Tidal Basin." As I was reading, I felt wonder and amazement at the cycle of the cherry blossom trees that bloom year after year at Tidal Basin in Washington, DC. In her poem, Cynthia shows her readers this cycle through the different things that happen to the blossoms during a season and how the cycle keeps going year after year.

Cynthia decided that she wanted her readers to feel like they were surrounded in a world of cherry blossoms when reading her poem. In order to do this, she decided to show people in her poem experiencing the blossoms. Her original poem mentioned soldiers returning from combat. Her revised poem now also mentions children and tourists, too. By adding these other people into her poem, she gives her readers more sets of eyes through which to see the blossoms. This means that when people read her poem they will be better able to feel what it's like to be at Tidal Basin during cherry blossom time.

When revising for the heart of the poem, first try to figure out what the big idea of your poem is. Then,

think about how you want your poem to make people feel. Do you want your poem to make people laugh or smile or be amazed? Or maybe, like Cynthia, you want to transport your reader to a certain place and time and make your reader really feel what it would be like to be there. Once you figure out what you want them to feel, then you can add details that will help you accomplish this goal.

Happy revising!
Mandy Davis

Mandy Davis is the author of the middle-grade novel *Stuperstar*, which will be published by HarperCollins in the fall 2016. She received her BA in Education from Purdue University and her MFA in Writing for Children and Young Adults from Hamline University. Before becoming a writer, she spent her time as an elementary school teacher where her favorite subject to teach was always writing. When she's not writing or teaching others, she can usually be found in the kitchen trying a new recipe or sitting around a table playing a board game. She also loves singing and trying to accompany herself on instruments like the accordion, the banjo, and the ukulele (but not all three at the same time).

Cynthia Wang

Cynthia is a third grader at Argonaut Elementary School. Math is her easiest subject, but she likes writing the best. Her class has a guinea pig named Humphrey, and Cynthia is looking forward to taking him home for the weekend. Cynthia likes playing soccer and Minecraft, a computer game. For Cynthia's next writing project, she will be writing a speech to try to convince her school principal to install Minecraft on the school computers.

Here are some of Cynthia's thoughts on the writing and revision of "Cherry Blossoms at Tidal Basin."

What was your favorite part of the revision process?

I liked coming up with more lines and helping readers understand more about my poem.

What advice do you have for other Inklings who don't like revision very much?

Revising is just a way to make your story or poem better. You might have other ideas that will add more to your story. But remember, the story is yours. You don't have to change things if you don't want to.

When did you start writing and what do you write now?

I started writing early pieces with my crayons when I was little. I would mostly draw pictures and write a few simple words. In school, I write in a really descriptive way. In a persuasive piece like "We Need More Playground Balls," I might start the piece with something funny. I always try to make my writing interesting.

Why do you enjoy writing?

Writing to me is a way of life. When I have a full imagination, I go to a notebook and start writing what I see. Once on my trip to Utah, I looked outside and it gave me more than a page to write about.

How do you come up with your ideas?

I can have an idea anywhere. If someone tells me to look at a tree, I observe it and write something descriptive. I get my ideas from everywhere.

Cherry Blossoms at Tidal Basin

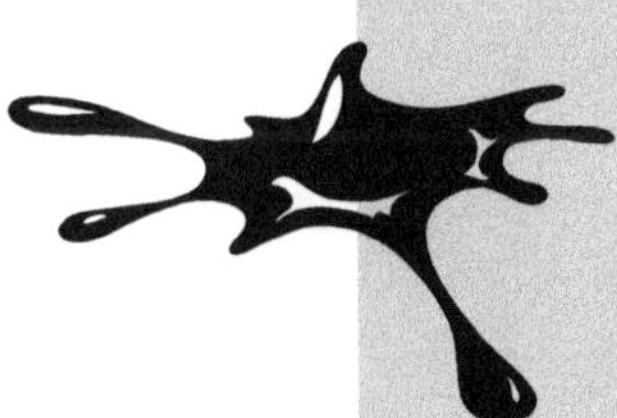

by

Cynthia Wang

260

Up upon a hill, cherry blossoms bloom,

Under the silvery glow of the moon.

Blossoms bloom, pink, white, and little,

Delicate, fragile, and so brittle.

White insides, pink outsides, what a sight to see!

Beautiful cherry blossoms, don't you quite agree?

Sweet air wafts past like a breath of a bee,

While a child runs a finger over me.

Tourists come and go, blinding me with light,

The Milky Way shimmers down all through the night.

A tiny bulb peeks out, new to the world,

While wind breezes on flowers making them twirl and whirl.

Swaying to the wind, like a little dance,

Being blown up and down, like a horse's prance.

Cherry Blossoms At Tidal Basin

Look at the great cherry blossom mat,

Did the soldiers visit, even from combat?

Falling, falling, falling, watch that blossom go!

Gently landing on the melting snow.

On the snow, the flower soon decays,

But somewhere under the blossom, a sprout is at bay.

What a cycle started 100 years ago,

And yet the tree still stands to grow and grow.

Putting the Details in Order

Sarah Lyn Rogers worked with Daniel Kao on guiding the reader through his poem, "The Tree," by bringing an order to the vivid details he includes.

Dear Reader,

Even before revision, Daniel's poem, "The Tree," contained some sophisticated poetic devices. Daniel has a great ear as a young poet! His interest in sound play showed through alliteration ("roots ripple") and internal rhyme ("giant winding"), choices that made his poem sound musical.

The first draft of "The Tree" had vivid imagery, too—like "scars healing on the bark"—but the details weren't in a specific order. The first stanza focused on the tree's bark. The next stanza was about the leaves, followed by the grasses around the tree, the roots, then the branches, and finally the trunk.

Even though poems don't have to tell a story with a beginning, middle, and end, they make for a better read when they have a clear structure. With Daniel, I talked about different strategies for putting his details in order.

He could start at the top of the tree, at the leaves, and work down to its roots—or the other way around.

He could start in the inside of the tree, at the roots and trunk, and then focus out to the grasses that surround it—or the other way around.

There's no single best way to put details in order. If you're not sure where to start, think about where you want your poem to end. In other words, what's the last thing you want your readers to see or hear? Daniel decided to end with the roots and the soil so that he could close on this line: "for even when mankind has run itself into the ground / you will still be there."

When you think about details, don't forget point of view. The first draft switched back and forth from third-person narration about the tree ("the tree… stoically endures") to second-person narration to the tree ("your leaves give me life"). It wasn't clear when or why the narration would switch. This is pretty common in early drafts of poetry, and something to look for in your own work.

In the finished poem, Daniel sets the scene with a third-person stanza and addresses the rest of the poem directly to the tree. This choice is one solution, and a refined one at that. My advice for Daniel, and for you, is to make a change and see how it feels. More than one structure can work—but you have to restructure with purpose!

Happy revising,
Sarah Lyn Rogers

Sarah Lyn Rogers is a self-described dorky grammarian, cat-lady, and retro clothing enthusiast. Sarah is also an MFA candidate at San José State University, where her emphases are fiction and poetry. Completing her trio of art degrees are a BA in Creative Arts and an AA in Studio Art. When she's not writing for herself or working with Young Inklings, Sarah is an assistant fiction editor for The Rumpus.

Daniel Kao

Daniel is a seventh grader at Ascencion Solorsano Middle School. He loves to doodle and read. Although he doesn't mind a trip to the woods once in a while, he much prefers city life, despite getting most of his inspiration for his poems from nature. Daniel's favorite food is sushi and he loves a nice swig of strawberry lemonade now and then. His favorite animal is a mourning dove because it has a beautiful sounding call.

Here are some of Daniel's thoughts on the writing and revision of "The Tree."

Now that you've revised your poem, what's different about it?

If you see the poem that I started with and the final, finished poem, you will see that the original poem is much messier in terms of structure, point of view, grammar, etc. The finished poem is neater and has more precise language.

How has the revision process helped you as a writer?

The revision process really helped me realize that there are many ways a poem can be successful; it helped me realize that it really is up to the writer on which path to take.

When did you start writing?

I started writing when I was in first grade, when I wrote a picture book about two frogs.

Are you working on any new stories or poems right now?

I am working on two poems right now, both still in the early, prototypical stages.

What advice do you have for other young writers?

My advice for other young writers is to just write poems or stories to your heart's content. Sooner rather than later, you will probably stumble upon an exceptional piece of literature, and then you can further develop it to suit your needs. Also, pay attention to the little stuff, like grammar and spelling. Unless you are trying to make a point, try to read over your poem to see if you made a mistake, because those tiny mistakes can add up.

The Tree

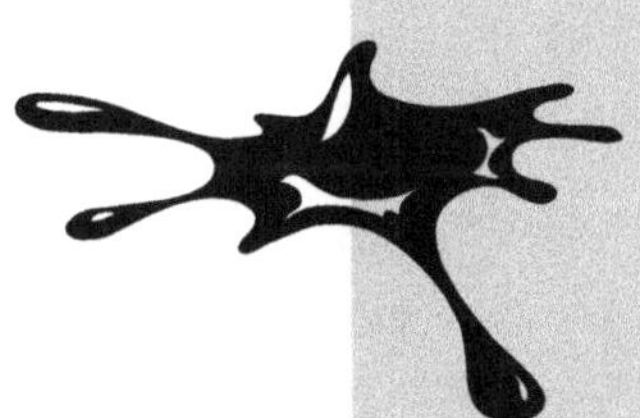

by

Daniel Kao

270

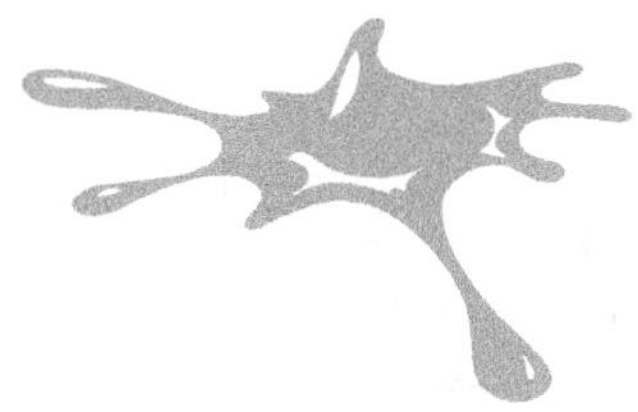

The tree.
never moving
stoically endures the torment of torturing tattoos
the endless "I was here" or names carved on;
the scars healing on the bark
for all to see

The branches on you strain forever up
shaped like crooked umbrellas
stretching into the skies
for kids to climb
like a stairway to the clouds and
giving shade on hot summer afternoons
even starting as foundations for future tree houses

The Tree

Your leaves give me life-
for nothing can live without the pure air
that comes from you.
The grasses all around you sway, as if admiring your resilience,
because everybody has heard of trees that
even after furious infernos of flaming fires
grow from the ashes
rising resiliently

Your trunk
supports the whole tree
giving the ideal leaning spot for
panting joggers and excited squirrels alike
holding up the world

Your roots ripple from the ground curving~
like giant winding snakes
going this way and that
burrowing into the earth
unveiling priceless mysteries
that no one can solve
for even when mankind has run itself into the ground
you will still be there

Form

Patricia Pinedo worked with Evie Landreth on how to play with form to bring out new meaning in her poem, "What Others Couldn't Dream."

Dear Reader,

In this revision, I focused on the form of the poem with Evie. I think that she has some great rhyming lines and these are the moments that really stand out in the poem. I think you will notice it too, how the rhyming tends to add to the rhythm of the poem itself.

Her rhyming led me to believe that this poem could benefit from trying on different styles of form in order to see what other words or rhymes might help with the rhythm of the piece. I noticed that "What Others Couldn't Dream" was strong in rhymes, and decided it would be best to see how the form might work to enhance the overall message.

First, I had her try and use the Sonnet form on the poem. Using some of the same lines and phrases, we tried to make her poem fit into the sonnet rhyme scheme. During this process, we tried to stick to the Sonnet limits, and only broke them as we saw fit.

Second, I had her try to use the Villanelle form. This is actually one of my favorite forms of poetry that I like to use whenever I want to start a rhyming piece of poetry! I thought it could benefit this poem because of the underlying haunting quality that it has. A great example of this form is "Do Not Go Gentle Into That Good Night" by Dylan Thomas.

Third, being that we compacted her poem to fit into these two forms, now was our chance to break all the rules. I asked Evie if there were new rhymes she had not thought of. Perhaps even more rhymes or lines that could be added to the poem itself. This was the time to really play with the poem and see what could be added or taken away. It is always fun to write in a restricted form and then break all the rules and create your own new identity!

By branching out into different forms, the poem was forced into different ways of expression and was able to grow into a new type of poem or interpretation. Poetry is the earliest form of the written and verbal word, and has a long history. In order to grow as future poets from that history, we must appreciate where our roots started, in rhyme and form.

I hope you will enjoy and appreciate Evie's ability to embellish on these ancient forms and create something new and inspiring for all to read.

Happy Writing,
Patricia

Patricia Pinedo earned her B.A. in Literature with an emphasis in Creative Writing-Poetry from UC Santa Cruz. Her poetry has been published in literary journals. She completed her Masters in Fine Arts in Creative Writing at San Jose State. She has been a substitute teacher for the past four years, and has worked with a wide range of grade levels. Patricia is excited to be working with Society of Young Inklings, helping young students develop their storytelling and writing skills.

Evie Landreth

Evie Landreth is an eleven year old, and lives in Palo Alto, CA. She attends Jordan Middle School where her favorite subjects are language arts and science. She had been active in horse riding and enjoys sailing and writing poetry and prose. She is a fantastic poet with a bright future of writing ahead of her.

Here are some of Evie's thoughts on the writing and revision of "What Others Couldn't Dream."

What do you think changed the most when you started to use rhyme and rhythm in your poem?

Well, I found the poem altogether flows a lot better than what I had done with it.... (tech break) I thought my poem altogether flowed a lot better than how I wrote and it is a lot deeper and has a lot more meaning than how I wrote it before. And I think it just works a lot better because it seems like a real poem rather than a bunch of words that I put onto a page.

When I first told you about how to work with rhyming, were you excited about that, were you not excited, how did you feel about that?
I got a bit confused but I got a little bit more excited once I realized what it was and how I could do it. Because I had never really tried out any of this before. So I thought it would be interesting to try it and it turned out good.

Do you feel like your poem has changed meaning in any way?
Well, it still has the same meaning but it just has better words to help explain it. But no, I don't think it has really changed meaning, it is pretty much the same.

Why do you like to write?
Well, I think writing explains more. It helps me explain better than my spoken words, I am not very good with words sometimes and I think writing is a better way to explain myself. I have read poems that are so powerful and I thought, if only I could do that. That is when I started and I thought it would be fun.

Who is your favorite poet? Do you have a favorite?
No, not really. I read certain poems online but I never really capture the authors. I saw some poets on Instagram and stuff, but they're not like official poets but they are really good. So I guess them, but I don't really know.

**What advice would you give other writers, especially about the
revision process?**

Well, if you keep revising and you find the smallest mistakes and keep
improving your words. And just over view it a million times, not a
million times of course not. But if you keep looking it over and keep
sharing it to other people, your story, your poem, everything, it will
improve and you will become a better writer or poet yourself. I think
the revision process is actually really fun no matter how boring it may
seem. But you get to improve on what you thought was perfect. I think
that is really fun.

Are you writing anything right now?

Well, unless you count stuff in school, not really. I wrote like a fantasy
thing, so I guess that kind of counts. I have a bunch of old stories I
look back on, but I am not really working on anything new.

Short stories?

Yeah, I want to try and write a book but it's so hard to scrape ideas
together. So I just have a bunch of small ideas here and there that I
always go back to and look at.

What Others Couldn't Dream

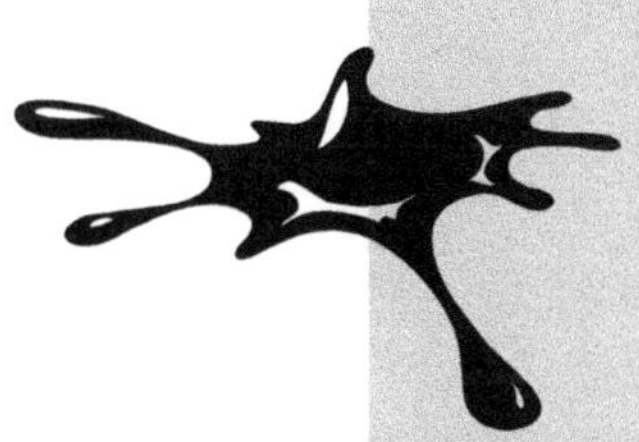

by

Evie Landreth

280

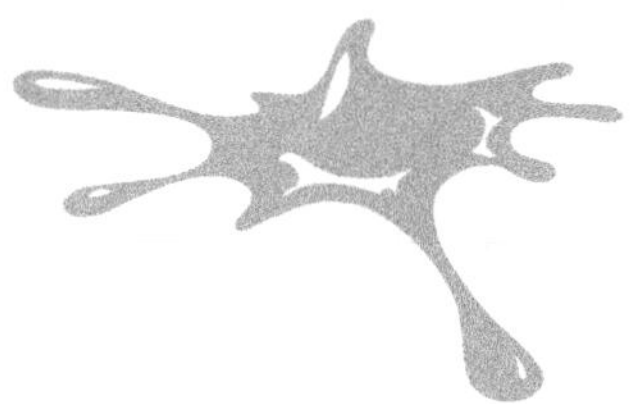

I paint the wrists of those who grieve

of those who can't remember

Why they are here and whether they should leave.

They can be short, tall, skinny, wide

But there is nothing wrong about them.

As you can see, I'm only their guide.

It just so happens that they have felt or seen,

what others couldn't dream.

They do not want to be here...

and wonder what's ahead.

So they shrink and disappear,

And, sadly, want to leave instead.

What Others Couldn't Dream

But let me tell you something,

there is much more to see and feel,

In spite of what they have felt or seen

You are beautiful.

With a sharp mind

and oh so kind.

You are not broken,

you just have seen the other side.

What others couldn't dream.

Life is a trial,

with twisted thoughts,

Confronting denial.

But if you are still here,

even with painted wrists and a shattered heart,

you have already won.

You are not broken.

WHAT OTHERS COULDN'T DREAM

Building Towards an Ending

Erica McCuaig worked with Katie Turk on bringing closure to her poem, "From Seed to Tree," by focusing on building towards an ending.

Dear Reader,

Katie's poem evokes some beautiful images, but it also hints at a deeper message. Much is left for the reader to interpret, and that magical conversation between author and reader begins.

What I love about "From Seed to Tree" is its simplicity. Who doesn't know the stages of growth for a tree? And yet, who stops to take the time to appreciate the simple, awe-inspiring beauty of that process?

As a revision focus, we chose building toward an ending. Katie altered the poem's ending to convey a greater sense of closure and peace. This leaves the readers in the right frame of mind to ask themselves what they will truly take away from this poem. As part of this process, Katie actually wrote several possible endings to the poem, then went through them to select the strongest choice.

It's important for writers and readers to remember that just because a poem seems simple, that doesn't mean it was simple to write. Often authors tweak and revise poems at length in order to get them to the point where they convey their messages in the most simple and effective way possible.

Readers could divine any one of a number of messages from this poem. One might think about the importance of taking a moment out of his/her hectic, modern, technology-driven life to glory in the wonders of nature. Another might be reminded of the simple truth that all life is a process, and is ever evolving. A reader might even feel a sense of gratitude for the peace that sometimes only Mother Nature can provide.

I like to imagine that Katie observed a massive, sprawling tree with innumerable branches and armies of leaves, and that her reaction was to remind herself that it was once even smaller than she is now. The idea fills me with a sense of respect, humility, gratitude, and above all—possibility.

There is no one right answer. The reader is free to find the meaning that he or she needs most. What we can all agree on is that just like the seed in her story, this young author is full of potential.

Happy Reading,
Erica

Erica McCuaig graduated summa cum laude with a BA in Psychology. Over the next few years, Erica taught preschool, middle school, and high school. She also worked with children of all ages as a tutor, mentor, nanny, behavior therapist, and instructor. Throughout that time, she wrote several collections of poetry and began developing her writing portfolio. Erica is now proud to work for the Society of Young Inklings as an Instructor and Mentor. She is excited to be able to further develop her skills and passion for writing while helping children find their own.

Katie Turk

Katie is a California native, and has lived in the same home her whole life. She began writing poetry in kindergarten, and continues to enjoy it to this day! She loves writing all forms of poetry and stories, as well as working on her art. Katie is also a Girl Scout, amateur computer programmer, beach lover, and math enthusiast. A young lady of varied interests and talents, she brings enthusiasm and an independent spirit to all of her pursuits.

Here are some of Katie's thoughts on the writing and revision of "From Seed to Tree."

When did you first start writing?

That's a hard question. I think I started writing poems around kindergarten.

Do you prefer writing poetry over stories?

I like writing both the same, but some people think I'm better at poems than stories. I say I'm good at both equally. Once I wrote a story that was completely in rhyme. That was fun.

When writing a poem, do you start with a structure or a subject?

I give myself a minute to think, and then I write about the first word that comes into my head. Sometimes when I'm looking up rhymes in a rhyming dictionary, I see a word that I like better and write a poem about that instead!

Do you like to experiment with different types of poems?

Most of the time I just write poems where every other line rhymes, but I like to experiment with others too. Currently I'm trying to write a poem called a thirteener. A thirteener must have thirteen lines, each with thirteen syllables, and it is very challenging!

Do you have a favorite poet or poem?

I like lots of different poets, but if I had to choose a favorite, I would probably pick Robert Frost.

Are you working on any new projects now?

I always am! Currently I'm trying to put together a book of poetry. Also, I want to write a series—by kids, for kids!

Do you like to share your work, or do you usually prefer to keep it private?

I like keep my work private until it is finished, and then when I'm done I like to share it with some other people.

Is it easier to write for school or yourself?

Personally, I like to be able to write using my own ideas. It can be hard to have to follow directions, especially since I think when you are writing poetry you should be able to let your imagination run free. I find it better to think outside the box.

Are you ever surprised by how a poem turns out?

Well, sometimes poems turn out differently than I expected. But since poetry has no rules, I don't mind.

Do you have a favorite subject matter for your poetry?

No, although my poetry seems to reflect my mood. I think that's a good thing, because it's important that you can talk to someone somehow if you don't want to talk face-to-face.

From Seed to Tree

by

Katie Turk

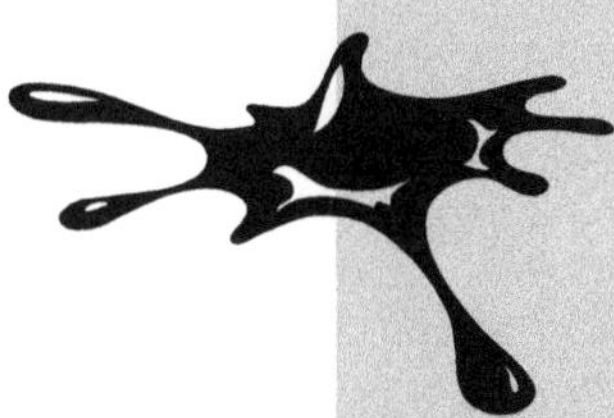

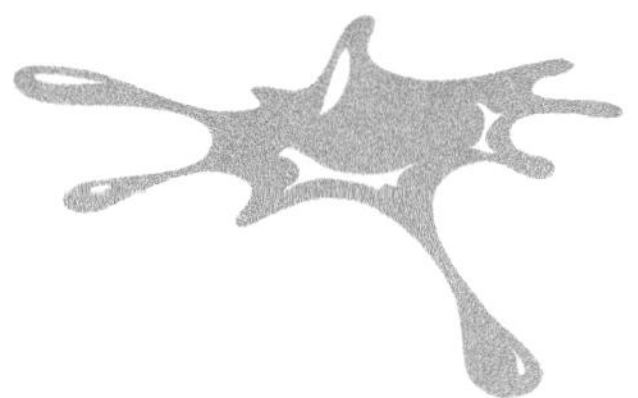

A seed in the dirt,

Buried in the ground

Ready for its inner

Tree to be found.

A sprout growing outwards

From a seed so small,

Ready to grow

And become bold and tall

From Seed to Tree

A sapling still growing

Quite rapidly,

Nicely taken care of

By gardener me

Now an oak stands tall

For all to see

As a gentle breeze blows

Swaying its leaves

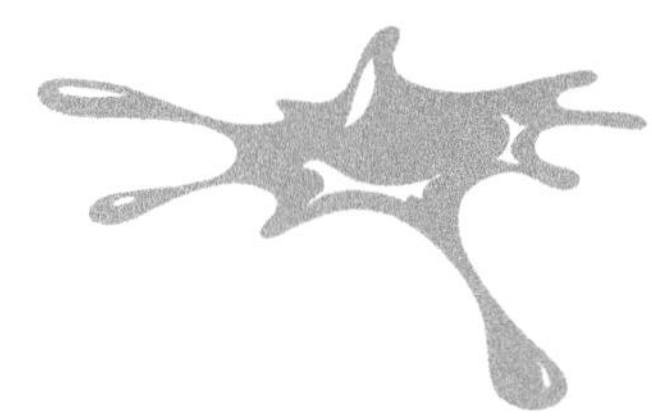

Theme Continuity

Marilyn Hilton mentored Samantha Sasaki through a revision focused on consistently communicating a theme throughout her poem.

Dear Reader,

When I read Samantha's "100 Shades of Summer," I was stirred by the beautiful imagery, believable details, and strong, tenderhearted character. I was also moved by the theme within the story of the poem. It was so powerful that Samantha and I talked about revising the poem to strengthen the theme's continuity.

You might ask: What does continuity of theme

mean? Let's use a tree for illustration. The thickest part of a tree is its trunk, which stands upright because it's supported by its roots. A tree also has branches, which grow leaves that draw sunlight and carbon dioxide for nourishment. Without roots and leaves, the tree would not stay healthy, and in time it would die. All parts of the tree work together, no part of the tree is wasted, and everything makes sense. (By contrast, a birch tree with pine needles wouldn't make sense.)

In a poem (or story), you can think of the theme as the tree trunk; like a trunk that runs the length of a tree, you can see where the theme is repeated, illustrated, foreshadowed, challenged, and so on throughout the poem. All elements of the poem—the language, action, imagery, conflict, story arc, visual structure, and so on—support the theme, and each part fits logically and makes sense. This is theme continuity. Often we don't know what the theme of a poem or story is until after we've written it. And then we can figure out how we can revise to support and strengthen the theme. Here are some ways that Samantha revised her poem for continuity of theme:

- Removed or trimmed lines or whole sections or stanzas that weren't necessary. (Samantha courageously removed the first stanza and the last line of her draft for the final version.)

- Replaced words that foreshadowed, echoed, or alluded to the theme.

- Condensed text to tighten the language and remove words that cloud the theme.

- Added or refined imagery that supported the theme.

- Chose one metaphor, instead of several, to run throughout the poem (but she explored describing various dimensions of that metaphor).

Samantha's final poem was even stronger, more cohesive, and more powerful than the original draft. Try revising your next poem or story using the points above and see if you notice a difference.

Happy writing!
Marilyn

Marilyn Hilton has published poems and short stories in various journals and anthologies, and is the author of the middle-grade novels *Full Cicada Moon* and *Found Things*. She holds an MA in English/creative writing and works as a technical editor for a major software firm.

Samantha Sasaki

Samantha is an eighth grader at The Girls' Middle School in Palo Alto. She loves reading, acting, and writing, and plays a multitude of different sports. Her favorite authors currently include Maggie Stiefvater and Cassandra Clare, but the new classics like *Harry Potter* will always remain in her heart. "100 Shades of Summer" is her first published work (unless you count the ones in her head), and she's so excited to share it with you!

Here are some of Samantha's thoughts on the writing and revision of "100 Shades of Summer."

What inspired you to write this poem? How did you come up with the idea for "100 Shades of Summer"?

When I set out to write this, I wanted to write a poem in free verse because I had been experimenting with different styles of poetry. I knew I wanted to write a poem about a girl who saw the world differently, who was different from others, and the challenges she faced. At first I thought she'd have synesthesia, which is a confusion of the senses. But then I found out about a condition called visual agnosia, and knew that was what Summer had.

What process did you use to revise your poem? How did you make the decisions you did to revise?

I went through the comments my mentor made and I thought about how the changes would affect the story, tone, and voice I was trying to go for. And then I chose the comments that felt right to make and that would still preserve what I wanted the poem to be.

What were the easiest and the most difficult parts of revising this poem?

The easiest part was finding the pieces I knew I wanted to change and making those changes first. The hardest part was telling myself I needed to work on the revisions. So I made the smaller changes that would have the biggest effect first, but then the revisions got harder and harder to make.

What are your thoughts about revision in general?

Revision is good because you can step back after you've written it all. You can give yourself another chance to work on it by going back over your work and making it the best you can make it.

What are you working on now?

I'm working on a novel that I'm writing with the help of a mentor from Young Inklings. We meet every few weeks. It's a science fiction novel in two points of view, about time travelers—two kids who travel back to the earthquake in 1906. It has historical elements but it's mostly contemporary.

What advice do you have for other writers?

I would say to never give up. In the writing process, there are so many times where I feel stuck and get into a funk for days, but I've learned that you can't let that stop you from writing and thinking. I feel like if you have a story to write, write it, edit it, and keep at it until it is how you imagine it.

100 Shades of Summer

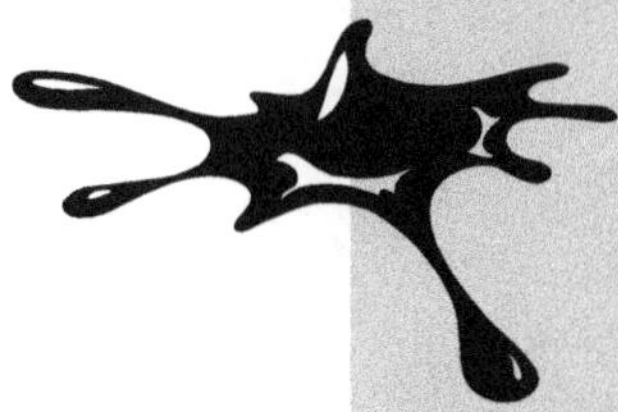

by

Samantha Sasaki

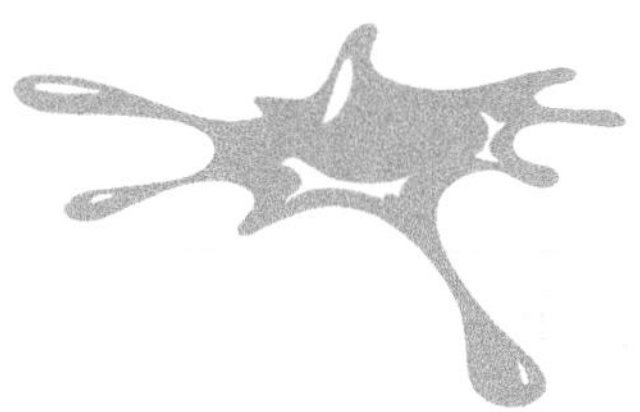

For me, the world is

a series of squiggles

and blobs

and swirls.

I can't tell a pencil

from a flower

A leaf is not a leaf

It's:

Drops

of dew hanging

on the bow of the green boat

Diamonds in the

light.

Not the big picture.

Everything is either

simplified

or

broken

Giant swathes of color

spread across an infinite canvas

or

tiny

shards

of

glass.

A puzzle

that I can't

put back together.

Official diagnosis: visual agnosia.

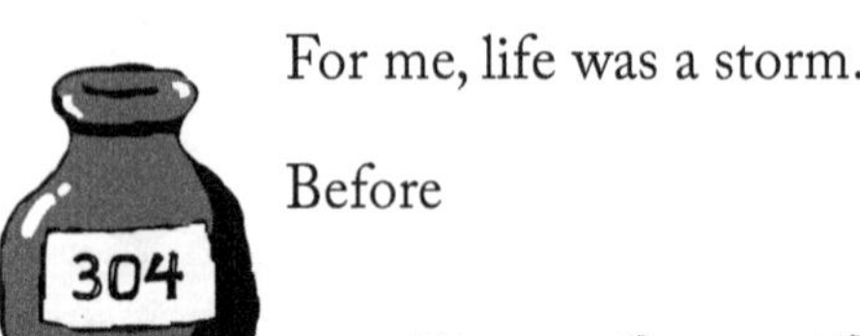

For me, life was a storm.

Before

my father lost his job,

my mother had to work,

home-schooling was no longer an option,

that was the calm.

The gentle peace lulling me

to sleep.

The false sense of security

that lets me forget what's to come.

Then the storm hit

and I started to drown:

I never realized

how cruel people could be

to those

who

were

different.

On the first day,

I stood outside

the classroom door,

five minutes before the bell.

100 Shades of Summer

Tick tock went my watch.

Clunk clonk went my heart.

My brain was buzzing with bees.

So was my stomach

my heart

my skin.

I was ready.

      I wasn't.

I was going in.

        I couldn't.

My mother kissed my forehead

and told me have fun!

Even though her voice

quivered

wobbled

    shook

But my choice had been made.

My classroom is like

    a fruit basket.

    Students stacked in rows

and sometimes spilling out

each with their own little variation and color

that tells you what's inside.

But they're a lot harder to read than a fruit basket

and a lot less delicious.

Before:

stayed up studying

the shapes and lines and angles

of the classrooms

so

I wouldn't call a desk

a pillow.

Now:

Everything blurred together

and swirled together

and White expanse jarring against

a hideous blue. Sheet? Snow?

WHAT?

filled my mind until I

     couldn't

think

straight

anymore.

this is too much

Until I found myself

next to the teacher

who's the shortest man the world

has ever seen.

Class, he said, his voice a badly tuned piano

Summer will be joining us for the remainder of the year.

If she needs any help, please do so.

I noticed he said nothing

about my condition.

Why?

64 bright dots of color:

all turned towards me

trapping me in their gaze.

I smiled

or waved

or laughed

And suddenly

I'm free.

In the box of fruit,

or was it chocolates?

there is one piece missing:

a piece in the back next

to a boy who looks like a kiwi,

with dark, dark hair

and green, green eyes.

I sat down next to him.

He didn't avert his gaze from the

white square stamped on the desk and the

black squiggles running across the page.

A yellow thing was in his hand

poised to attack with its stinger

A bee, I shrieked in terror.

Why hadn't he dropped it yet?

The girl next to me,

an apple with dark red hair

100 Shades of Summer

and death white skin,

started to

      scream

         scream

            scream

until she saw what was in

Kiwi's hand

and started to

      sneer

         laugh

            jeer

at me.

Can't you see that's a pencil, Summer?

Her voice was a knife

that cut through all my hopes

of ever fitting in.

A pencil

      A pencil

A pencil

      bounced around the room

      punctuated with a laugh.

My eyes stung and I put my head on the pillow.

And even though

the teacher reprimanded the class

and sort of apologized,

that didn't change that to them

I was a freak.

A paper nudged my arm

and I saw the edge of

white snow with swirls of demon blood

dancing around on it.

Kiwi's head appeared next to mine

and he mouthed I'm sorry

and for the first time

I could see what the picture was of:

a classroom filled with kids

with winged pencils flying around their heads

and writing Long live Summer with little bees.

I didn't know if he said sorry for the class

or if he thought the picture

could have been mean,

but I smiled anyway because

he drew Apple with an apple head

as well.

I drew a sloppy kiwi on his head

too

and we laughed and drew and I thought

Maybe I have a friend.

And I guess the rest of the day

went OK

except it was just so obvious

how different I was from

everyone else.

The things I knew

      the way I explained things

            my visual agnosia

And I just was so far away from everyone.

And I learned from the rest of the

      days

      weeks

        months

that

Apple (whose name was actually Lizzie)

was the worst

and Kiwi (Jeremy) was the best

and everyone else was in between

ranging from friendly

to disgusted

One day,

I had to go to the office to lie down

since everything I saw was

colors

        spinning

flashing

                too chaotic

and nothing made sense.

I saw Apple outside of there,

talking with a smear of black

against her head with

crystals running down her face.

It took me a while to realize

that she

was

crying.

She kept repeating

I'm sorry, I'm sorry

and cringing like she was being

physically hit by the sound

coming out of the smear.

And I realized that this girl

who bullied me

and teased me

relentlessly

had her own demons.

Could I hate her for that?

And as I stood there, pondering

Apple suddenly jerked her head up

staring

    right

              at

                me

Guilt and fear played tug-of-war

in my stomach

as I thought of some sort of response.

But Apple pulled the smear away

and put her head in her hands

and I felt my legs move

and

I

walked

over.

Apple didn't look up,

just kept sobbing into her hands.

I didn't say anything

just eased her head onto my shoulder

and held her while she cried.

I had never seen

anyone cry like that before

like their world was splintering apart.

But I didn't ask her what was wrong

and she didn't tell me

and we just sat there

until her tears dried up.

100 Shades of Summer

Why? she asked, getting up.

I got up too

wondering the same thing.

Because there's more to you than how you seem

and everyone needs a shoulder

to cry on. I told her simply.

She nodded and smiled

and slowly walked away.

We never talked about that

but we never were that much at odds again.

I think Kiwi knows though.

It's funny,

in a place where I thought

I would have no friends

is the place where people truly

understand me

and truly misinterpret me.

So I don't need to tell Kiwi

that everyone sees everyone

in their own way.

That even though there is one

Apple, she has so many sides

so many shades.

And that the same thing goes for me

and Kiwi

  and my parents

    and everyone.

Because there is 100 sides of me

and 100 sides of Kiwi and Apple and everyone

too.

It's just hard to see all of them.